D0363459

SOULS OF ANGELS

Also by Thomas Eidson

St Agnes' Stand
The Last Ride
All God's Children
Hannah's Gift

THOMAS EIDSON

Souls of Angels

HarperCollins*Publishers*

HarperCollins*Publishers*
77–85 Fulham Palace Road,
Hammersmith, London W6 8JB

www.harpercollins.co.uk

Published by HarperCollins*Publishers* 2006
1 3 5 7 9 8 6 4 2

Thomas E. Eidson asserts the moral right to
be identified as the author of this work

A catalogue record for this book
is available from the British Library

ISBN-10: 0 00 718174 4
ISBN-13: 978 0 00 718174 2

Typeset in Sabon by Palimpsest Book Production Limited,
Grangemouth, Stirlingshire
Printed and bound in Great Britain by
Clays Ltd, St Ives plc

This novel is entirely a work of fiction.
The names, characters and incidents portrayed in it are
the work of the author's imagination. Any resemblance to
actual persons, living or dead, events or localities is
entirely coincidental.

This book is proudly printed on paper which contains wood
from well managed forests, certified in accordance with
the rule of the Forest Stewardship Council
please visit www.fsc-uk.org

FSC

For Cathy, my wife

SOULS OF ANGELS
Los Angeles 1882

Only God
*Mexican graffito scratched into the wall of a
Los Angeles jail, 1880s*

ONE

It was late, somewhere past three in the morning. She was making her way through the darkness shrouding the old plaza, following the main brick pathway that twisted and turned through overgrown oleanders and scrub oaks and mountains of Castilian roses. The town was silent, the sky deep ebony without a moon, the landscape only faintly illuminated by the glow of the new gas lamps that fringed the hundred-year-old gardens like amber beads on a necklace. Storm clouds were coming in from the north. Somewhere in the distance a dog howled and a coyote yipped an answer, and she shivered in the cool air and walked faster.

She had been with one of her regular customers and was half-drunk and angry because the man had ripped her new dress. She pulled the hem up close to her face and walked on, squinting to see the tear in the material, swearing under her breath. The dress had cost a week's work. She let the material drop and touched gently at the small bruise on her cheek, then stopped and pulled a hand mirror and rouge from her bag and tried to see herself in the moonlight, straightening her hair and patting colour over the sore spot. Dorothy Regal was twenty-four years old, though she appeared no more than sixteen – the mercy of Providence, she liked to say. She was staring into the glass wondering how much longer she could sell herself as a child, when something moved in the darkness behind her – her eye just catching a blur of motion in a corner of the little mirror. Her breath reversed in her throat.

'Hello?' she called softly, not wanting an answer.

There was none.

She started walking again, faster and with more purpose, assuring herself that the movement had been made by one of the town's cur dogs hunting garbage left by picnickers. Even so, it wasn't smart being in the plaza this late. Nervous in a way that she didn't fully understand, Dorothy stopped once more and turned in a slow circle and searched the surrounding blocks of shadows. She could see nothing unusual.

The stars were bright in the sky over the darkened town, the gardens quiet and beautiful, the clouds edging closer. She did not see a figure slipping away through the shadows. But she sensed the movement. For the past month she'd had this same feeling. She didn't know who or why. There was just the unease.

Dorothy took a deep breath, then began walking again, drawing her shawl tightly around her. She left the darkness of the plaza and crossed Olive Street, heading north, and turned onto the wide dirt street that was called La Calle del Negro by the Mexicans. Shivering once more, she wrapped her arms around her thin shoulders. She could feel the rainstorm approaching in the cool night air, coming in as it always did during this season from the Tehachapi Mountains to the north, driving the smell of the deserts ahead of it.

Someone was playing a piano badly in one of the few establishments still open and she could hear weary laughter from a window above her. While she had calmed a bit, she kept moving. She was chilled and tired and wanted sleep.

The road and sidewalks before her were empty. A few lanterns hung outside the buildings, casting dull puddles of yellow light onto the ground, and both sides of the street were lined with bars, bagnios and Chinee caves. Knowing that the Americans ran the liquor and gambling, the Mexicans the bordellos and the Orientals the opium, she wondered how the place ever came to be called La Calle del Negro.

She stopped in front of a two-storey wood-frame boarding house, La Fiesta. She was home. At least the room upstairs in the back where she met customers and lived was a home of sorts. She touched at the bruise on her cheek, a momentary veil of melancholy dropping over her. Maybe she should just go back to her real home. But she shook her head at the thought, shook it hard enough to make her long metal earrings yank at the lobes of her ears. They would never have her back. Anyhow, she didn't even know if they were alive.

The rain was on her quickly and she pulled her shawl over her head and hurried down the darkened path between two buildings, trotting up the old wooden stairs and entering her room. There was no lock but she did have a wooden brace that she jammed at an angle between the floor and the doorknob. Finished, she felt better. She pulled her damp dress over her head and laid it out on the small bed. There was dirty wallpaper pasted over the window glass for her customers' privacy, creating a heavy darkness. The rain was pounding hard against the roof.

Something about the sound was comforting to her.

Dorothy Regal put her hand on the slight swelling of her belly, held it for a moment, then smiled and struck a match and lit the candle on the nightstand beside her bed. She waited for the small flickering flame to grow before she bent and began to carefully examine the tear in her dress. A moment later, she heard a clicking metallic sound behind her and she stiffened, then straightened up and slowly turned around. The figure was standing in a dark corner of the room, hatted and dressed in a black wrist-length cape, the hat's brim pulled low over the eyes. She squinted at what she could see of the features in the weak candlelight. There wasn't much. Her breath sounded like the wind through the old tree outside her window. And she was trembling.

Dorothy tried to compose herself, reasoning that most of her customers came to her room unannounced and wondering why this one should make her nervous. Her naked shadow lurched awkwardly like a puppet in the flickering candlelight wavering against the wall. Her eyes narrowed again. 'It's late,' she said.

The figure nodded as if in sympathy and stepped closer. Dorothy was trying to see the face beneath the brim of the hat, when something silvery flashed in the dull light like a minnow in a stream. She thought she had been spat on.

Then she was staring up at the ceiling.

TWO

Sister Ria sat alone inside the moving stagecoach thinking about the dead woman and avoiding the sunlight burning through a crack in the roof, the heat dragging up memories of summers past in this place. But she told herself for the thousandth time, she was not here for sentimental reasons.

She gazed out the window at a group of Mexican workers stacking orange crates in a small boat on a sandy beach. She hadn't eaten an orange since leaving St Augustine's nunnery in Spain, eight years before. Eight years. Could it have been that much time since Spain? It did not seem possible. So much in her life had changed. Not all of it for the best.

Sister Ria of the Benedictine Order of the Sisters of Mercy had been travelling for almost two months now from her convent in Poona, India. Days after she had received the cable informing her of the charges against her father, and after the health officials had let her go, she had made her way to the port city of Bombay where she caught a tramp steamer to England. She squirmed on the seat. The very thought of her father made her uneasy. And try as she might she could not drive this feeling from her. All she could do was keep reminding herself that she had not come back because of him. She had come for only one reason, to fulfil the promise that she had made as a child to her dying mother that she would care for him. She shook her head at this troubling thought and looked out at the ocean.

With barely enough money and food to sustain her, it had been a difficult journey. But she had fasted longer and lived in far worse conditions. In the crowded harbour at Liverpool she had searched until she found a three-mast clipper headed for America and paid her passage by cooking meals on a huge wood-burning stove in the ship's galley. Then two weeks ago she had crossed the American continent, jammed in a Zulu-class compartment of the Union Pacific–Central Pacific railroad. Now she was sweating in the heat inside the mid-week coach from Monterey to Los Angeles, close to her destination.

The stage was rolling down a coastal road, high bluffs to her left, white sand and ocean on the right. It was lonely here. Beautiful but lonely. The Chumash Indians called this stretch of shoreline Malibu – *Where the Surf Sounds Loud.*

Sister Ria stared blindly at the pounding breakers, half-listening to the screeching gulls, and thinking back to summer days when she and her older sister, Milagros, and their nursemaids had played here. She had loved those days – away from the hacienda, away from him. But those days were gone and she was no longer a child.

She took a deep breath and held it, her eyes frozen on the water and sand. She had found God here on this very beach some thirteen years before. She was eleven years old that summer, her life shattered by the death of her mother and older brother, and the strange existence she had been forced into living with her father. They had come here – her older sister and their nursemaids – on that hot August day to picnic and play in the shallows of the surf. The old man, Manuel Escobar, had followed at a respectful distance on his horse, as he always did whenever they left the hacienda grounds. He waited on a bluff above the beach, watching them as if they were precious cargo.

She tensed on the seat of the coach remembering the sudden urge that had come over her to walk into the water and to keep walking, to end this life with him. She had waited until the others were eating the noontime meal, then she had waded out into the rolling waves – had been knocked down twice – but kept struggling until she was behind the rising swells of the breakers, her clothing weighing her down in the surging drift of the sea. When the water was up to her neck the old man had fired his pistol into the air and pointed at her and hysteria broke out among the young nurses who ran up and down the beach, begging her to return.

Her older sister had not begged her. Milagros had understood, had walked down to the edge of the water and watched her – and when she turned around for the last time, Millie had waved goodbye. Sister Ria shut her eyes and wiped the tears from her cheeks, remembering the bliss that had descended upon her as she submerged beneath the sea, drifting at peace in the green waters.

The voice had stopped her.

It gently called her name. And when she didn't respond it said her name again and seemed to shake her – as if a shark had grabbed her – and she burst above the water, gasping for air. God had spoken to her, she was absolutely convinced of it.

Sister Ria straightened the material of her habit over her knees and gazed out now at the surf, remembering the voice, so gentle, so loving and yet so frightening. 'You will serve me,' was all it had said. 'I have tried, Lord,' she whispered.

When she was thirteen she had paid a freighter to take her in his wagon, along with his load of chickens, to Santa Barbara, dropping her off at the Franciscan nunnery. But upon his return to Los Angeles the man had told her father what she had done, and he had come for her. She had run away again a year later to Guaymas, Mexico, to join a cloistered convent on the coast. But the sisters said she was too young and had the local priest write to him and he had sent the hacienda's head servant, Aba, to bring her home – back to the humiliation that was her life with him.

Three years later, at seventeen, she had fled this place for the last time, travelling a world away to Spain where she had given up her name, Isadora Victorine Lugo, and the few possessions she had with her and become a postulant of the Benedictine Sisters. Then on her eighteenth birthday she had taken her sacred vows and the name Sister Ria, leaving immediately for the order's convent in Poona. She had worked there in the mission hospital for four years – a region of death from typhoid, cholera and smallpox, but that had not frightened her because God had been with her. Nor had her choice three years ago when she and several other Sisters volunteered to live and work inside a walled and guarded village of lepers in an otherwise uninhabited valley outside the ancient city.

She had made her decision for her Lord. Even so, the last three years had not been easy. She took a deep breath

10

of the sea air and held it. The smell had been the worst of it. The foetid odour of the lepers' sores had made her nauseous. She had prayed that the sense of disgust for the rotting flesh would leave her . . . that she could receive this as though it were Christ. But it had not happened. She squeezed her hands together until her knuckles turned white.

Still, she had been doing God's work so it was bearable. 'Suffer joyfully,' Mother Superior Isabel would tell the sisters. 'God loves a cheerful giver.' What seemd almost unbearable was her return to this place. She continued to look out at the beach and the rolling waters where her epiphany had taken place.

I will do my best, Mother.

Exhausted, Sister Ria let her breath out and leaned back into the worn leather seat and listened to the sounds of the horses labouring in their traces. She said a small prayer to St Francis to lessen their exertions, then smoothed the long black material of her wimple with an awkward movement of her hands, making certain her face was properly framed, her neck covered by the white cloth of her couvre-chef. Rivulets of sweat were running down her back and over her buttocks. She clamped her knees together and sat working on what she would say to him.

As she sat debating with herself, something moved on the seat beside her and she jumped and saw an old yellow cat in the shadows. His ears were flattened, as if somebody had hit him over the head with a board, and he looked peeved at the world. She smiled. 'How did you get in here, *viejo* – old man?'

The cat didn't answer, he just meowed and tried to look dainty. But he was too big and rough looking to be convincing, and he was hurt, an eye freshly gouged out

11

and blood caked on his fur. She started to reach for him, sliding her hand slowly towards the animal, but he apparently did not like closeness and he spat and limped away across the seat. He looked badly beaten up. Sister Ria's face hardened into her best nursing countenance. 'I have to examine you,' she said, in a firm voice. The cat hissed and backed further away.

She eyed him carefully: he was very big and very ill-tempered looking. She drew a deep breath and in an even firmer voice said, 'You stay put. Do you hear me?' In response, the old tom arched his back and let forth a horrible sound from somewhere deep inside him. She shrugged as if she heard that same terrifying sound every day and was bored by it. 'Listen,' she continued. The cat spat once more as if to emphasize the awful things he was going to do if she persisted, then bared his sizeable fangs at her. 'I'm not afraid of you,' she lied.

Sister Ria raised a trembling hand and wiggled her fingers in the air like the legs of a tarantula. She watched the hand as if it belonged to someone else. The old cat watched it as well, teeth bared, ready to pounce. Then with a hard snap of the wiggling fingers, Sister Ria grabbed him behind his neck with her other hand.

He never had a chance.

It was late afternoon and Sister Ria had lowered the canvas curtains against the dust and sunlight. She was holding the old feline – whom she had christened Fernando after the Franciscan mission north of the pueblo – forcibly pinned down on her lap. He had just tried to bite her for the hundredth time and she tightened her grip on the scruff of his neck. Having completed her examination of his injuries, she was convinced none was fatal. He in turn seemed to be convinced she was mentally defective. He looked at her with his one eye as if to say as much.

Then, suddenly, the stagecoach's wheels slipped into deep sand and she forgot her little war with Fernando and pulled the window curtain up.

The driver was reining the sweating horses between heavy stone gate posts, slowing them to a prancing walk down a sandy drive bordered by ancient pepper trees, the drive turning and twisting until it led to an enormous house set back under towering sycamores. The house had the look of a Renaissance villa with heavy stone arches and colonnades, its white walls covered in beautiful flowering vines of wistaria and bougainvillaea.

When the coach stopped, Sister Ria of the Benedictine order of charitable nuns held the struggling Fernando out in front of her at a safe distance and stepped into the late afternoon heat. She fought the trembling in her body.

She was home.

THREE

The hacienda was cool and quiet and Sister Ria stood looking at it as if the heavy stuccoed walls might suddenly rush her. She could hear the coach moving away down the long drive and wished she was on it. Fernando lay momentarily still in her arms. She turned in a slow circle. Sister Ria had always known the house was beautiful, she had simply forgotten how beautiful.

The grand entry hall soared two storeys above her, the thick walls plastered the colour of a sun-ripened peach and textured in *rajueleado,* small, embedded stones covering the surface in dramatic patterns. In the centre of the entry was a low pool of water, a single spray rippling its still surface. The shadowy spaces looked arabesque.

She moved deeper into the house. The walls were painted in earthy, pale colours from dusty cream to melon, the ceilings braced with rough-hewn beams. There were baroque touches, giant gilt-wood mirrors and huge silver candelabras, contrasting with the delicate grace of French officers' chairs and other furnishings all distinctly different, all beautiful, all covered in fine fabrics of the same harmonious shades, all of it close to the patina of the old house. Her father was a genius with the hue and look of things. But that was his only act of genius.

She turned and entered a sparsely furnished room and stopped, her eyes fixed on a portrait of a woman and a boy that hung suspended by two long golden chains. The woman's smile touched something deep inside her, and tears began to fill her eyes. 'I came,' she whispered. Seeing them again – her mother and older brother Ramón – she wondered, as she always wondered: Why had the Lord taken them, leaving her with him?

She brushed the material of her habit as if trying to clear away her thoughts and knelt and prayed for their souls, then crossed herself and stood and reached up and touched the frame. Then she started walking again, fighting to maintain her grip on Fernando.

'This used to be my home,' she said to the old cat.

If he cared, Fernando did not show it.

Sister Ria walked on.

She had been born in this hacienda in the year 1857. The rancho was 37,000 acres of a Spanish land grant inherited by her father from his father, and named La Cienega after the marshlands at the foot of the Sierra Santa Monica. She had once believed it was a gift from God. She no longer had this feeling.

She stopped and listened.

The house was silent. The quiet reminded her of the mornings of her childhood when she would get up while the earth was still dark, and walk barefoot over the red tiles of the wide veranda, her feet numb from the cold floor, her head feeling light from the intense silence. She would stand looking at this world that belonged to her father, feeling that he might be a king of sorts. Yet she had learned that he was not a king. He was not even a good man. She winced at the thought and asked God to forgive her unkind acts of judgement, certain the Lord was growing tired of her constant backsliding. These were not the fair traits of a Sister of Mercy. Still, in her heart, she knew she was right.

Then Sister Ria heard footsteps and turned to see an old servant woman in a long black skirt and white blouse walking briskly down the main hallway towards her. The woman looked thin and grey, but not weak. She neither smiled nor seemed surprised at finding a nun with a cat in her arms standing in the great hall of the hacienda. She stopped and leaned on an ebony walking stick, looking as though she could put the stout tool to good purpose, and bowed slightly. 'May I help you?'

For a moment, Sister Ria just stood. Then she forgot herself and clutched the struggling Fernando tight against her and ran and threw an arm around the woman. 'Oh, Aba – Aba,' she cried.

The servant began to pull away.

'Aba, it's Isadora.'

The woman clamped a tiny pair of spectacles onto the narrow bridge of her nose and peered into Sister Ria's face. 'Child,' she said, putting a hand to the back of Sister Ria's head and pulling her into her shoulder. 'You are home.'

'You look wonderful,' Sister Ria said, bouncing on the balls of her feet. 'I've missed you so.'

The old servant's eyes moved slowly over Sister Ria's dark shapeless habit and the stark white bands framing her face. From the look in her eyes, Sister Ria was certain the woman was recalling the long, unpleasant trip she had made eleven years before to the convent at Guaymas to retrieve this stubborn child who stood before her now as a grown woman. 'Does he know what you have become?'

'No.'

'He will not be pleased.'

'It is no longer his place.'

'Isadora.' The woman's voice was sharp.

Sister Ria held the cat out as if he were a peace offering. 'His name is Fernando. He's hurt.'

Aba did not take him. Instead, she continued to eye Sister Ria's dark habit and the large wooden cross hanging at her side.

'Aba.'

Reluctantly, the servant tucked her walking stick under an arm and took hold of the old feline. Fernando stiffened as if he had been given a jolt of electricity, then he lashed out at Aba's thin hand before springing free, and bounding off into the depths of the house. The woman took an expert cut at him with her long black cane. She missed, but just.

'I will have him destroyed,' she said.

'Aba, don't tease.'

The woman turned and started down the loggia. 'Come with me, Isadora.'

Sister Ria wiped the dampness from her eyes and clasped her hands in front of her waist and followed in the slower walk of the convent, her eyes locked on the thin back of the old servant as if she were afraid the woman might disappear. 'Aba –'

'Not now.'

The loggia was paved in worn slate that followed the contours of the earth, the walls lined with floor-to-ceiling bookshelves, wall sconces spilling muted light in yellow pools down its cave-like length. Aba stopped in front of a heavy wooden door that looked ancient in the shadowy light. Sister Ria stopped a few feet behind her.

'Go ahead, Isadora.'

'He's not in jail?'

'Under arrest – but not in jail.'

'Did you know her?'

'Who?'

'Dorothy Regal?'

'Knock on the door, child.'

Sister Ria pulled herself up straighter and stepped forward and knocked softly. There was no answer. She knocked again. No sound came from the room.

'You have more strength than that, Isadora.'

She knocked harder. Still no response. She pushed down on the heavy brass handle and slowly opened the door. Then she heard the sharp tap of Aba's cane against the floor and turned back. The old woman stepped forward and placed her hands on Sister Ria's shoulders, and slowly turned her around until she was facing the open doorway again. 'You will show proper respect,' she said, straightening the coarse black material of Sister Ria's wimple.

'He is not the Pope, Aba.'

'You will show respect, child.' It was not a request. Then she adjusted the heavy material of the habit on Sister Ria's thin shoulders. 'Your robes are filthy.'

'I have been travelling.'

Aba brushed dust from the cloth. 'Regardless, you will show respect,' she repeated, smoothing a wrinkle with her thin hand. Then she again grasped Sister Ria's shoulders and squeezed gently. Sister Ria nodded and stepped inside.

The room was every bit as strange in appearance as she remembered. The windows were shuttered and the

18

long red drapes that spilled over the floor had been pulled shut over them, making the room as dark as the hallway. There was a candelabrum burning in the centre, tossing soft dancing light over everything. Her father had always loved the Muslim worlds of Afghanistan, Morocco and Persia, and his bedroom was filled with the trappings of these places, exotic silk fabrics and scimitars, hookahs, damask-covered cushions, Oriental tabourets, an exotic mixture of his personal fetishes. There was the smell of leather and scented oils, and wisps of incense hung in the air.

Even odder was the fact that the room was filled with baskets of fruit and candies and eggs. There were also bunches of flowers – some fresh, some dead – lying on the floor and hanging from the ceiling. And in hand-built willow crates stacked around the room were dozens of live rabbits, chickens and ducks, the smell of their droppings mixing with the sharp odour of incense. While offensive, the smell was nowhere near as suffocating as the stench of the dying lepers.

Sister Ria stood near the door and let her eyes adjust to the weak light of the room. 'Respect,' Aba said from the hallway. Sister Ria looked back at the old woman and curtseyed like a child and then felt bad, and said, 'Yes.'

She turned back to the room and stared at a small gold-painted table that supported the symbols of his odd collective sense of God: a crucified Christ, a sixteenth-century portrait of Buddha, a framed verse from the Koran. The sacristy of his life. Studying the Christ, Sister Ria tensed and crossed herself and then continued to look around the room. The bed was empty. He was nowhere to be seen. A large armoire stood open against one wall and she glimpsed his beautiful garments – bright tunics,

Afghans, jubbahs, kimonos – dozens of them. Then she saw him.

He was lying on a stone platform in a corner of the room dressed in a medieval Japanese suit of armour made of small lacquered pieces of bamboo laced together to form an apron-like skirt and another set of bamboo plates that draped like a stiff shawl over his back and shoulders.

'What are you doing, Father?'

'Contemplating my death.' His voice was weak and he looked thin, with deep sunken eyes underscored with black circles.

'I see,' she said, a sense of the old resistance creeping into her words, giving them an edge and surprising her after all these years, after all her prayers. She fought the feeling and in a calm voice, said, 'It is Sister Ria.' She caught herself and said, 'It's Isadora. I have –'

'Contemplate your death.'

'I am not here to contemplate.'

Suddenly, a hen in one of the cages began to cackle and the egg she had just laid slipped through the bottom slats and smashed onto the floor below. Sister Ria was looking for something to clean it up with when Don Maximiato Lugo began to stir. Slowly, as if it were a tremendous effort, he brought his thin legs over the edge of the coffin-like structure and pushed himself into a sitting position. He struggled to put on a metal samurai skullpiece with heavy leather flaps that protected his neck. She watched him. He looked unsteady, his head moving over his thin shoulders under the weight of the helmet, his deep-set eyes red, tearing and unfocused.

'It has been a long time, Father.'

He did not respond.

'You do not look well,' she said, finally.

20

He peered at her now with his head tilted at an odd angle.

She realized at that moment that he wasn't here, that he was lost in one of his drugged and senseless stupors. As if in response to her thoughts, a young Chinese boy entered the room carrying a tray with an opium pipe on it. He stopped when he saw her. She shook her head, then pointed towards the door. 'Please leave,' she said to the boy. 'There will be no more of that in this house,' she continued, sounding every bit the convent nurse.

'I will decide what will and will not take place in this house,' Don Maximiato snapped.

'Please leave,' Sister Ria said again. Then all the long years of caring for the sick and dying caused her to stiffen at the smell and sight of the filth in the room and she looked at the boy and said, 'Have these animals removed, and this room cleaned.'

Uncertain what to do, the boy set down the tray and bowed towards Sister Ria, then he bowed again, this time towards the old man, and began to scurry for the door.

'Young man,' she said.

The boy froze.

'Have you come to order me around?' Don Maximiato asked.

'No.'

The boy was turning back and forth from Sister Ria to her father.

'You have no right –'

'You are correct, I have no right.' She paused for a moment, 'May we give the animals to the workers?'

'No. They are sacred offerings.'

Sister Ria studied her father's face before turning slowly to the boy. 'Give them to the poor. To anyone in need.'

21

The boy bowed quickly and left.

The old man seemed to drift off again. His eyes had lost their focus and he looked as though he might fall over.

'I will pray for you. Whatever your affliction,' he mumbled, clasping his hands together.

'Do not pray for me, Father. Please – do not.' She stopped abruptly as if the words hurt.

Don Maximiato raised his head and looked at her, his eyes narrowing, his face flushing. Suddenly he seemed alert and aware of his surroundings.

'You will not tell me what I can and cannot do in my own house!' he shouted. He spun and picked up the tray with the opium pipe and flung these, smashing glass over the floor.

Sister Ria walked to the bed and leaned against a tall canopy post, looking at the back of her father's helmeted head, memories beginning to stir. 'After eight years,' she whispered. Suddenly her hands were shaking and she grasped the wooden post, squeezing with her fingers. 'You haven't changed. You never will.' Her voice was rising.

'Isadora,' Aba said through the open doorway.

Sister Ria had turned and started towards the old woman, when Don Maximiato said, 'I did not ask you to come here.'

She stared at him. His eyes were closed again. She cleared her throat and quietly said, 'No, you did not.' She studied his small face for what seemed a long time before she said, 'I came because I promised Mother I would come.' She paused. 'I came to ask you if you murdered that woman.'

He opened his eyes and looked up at her, scratching his chin as if perplexed.

'Please – don't jest. I do not deserve that,' she said.

He dismissed her with a wave of his hand.

Sister Ria continued to watch him for a time before she said, 'I'll wait for your answer,' then left the room.

Evening had come with a cold breeze laden with moisture from the sea. Sister Ria stood in the shadows of the loggia, looking out a window at the distant fields shading purple in the fading light. She was remembering things she didn't want to remember.

She smiled weakly. 'He is the same.'

Aba was standing behind her. 'He is your father,' she said.

'The things in his room –'

'Yes?'

'Why?'

'Some believe –' Aba said, crossing her arms over her breasts.

'Believe what?'

'That the Patrón is sainted.'

Sister Ria raised her eyebrows. 'Mad, perhaps . . .'

'He is the Patrón. He is your father. You will not speak of him in that manner.'

'In all my years with him, he never once called me daughter. Not once, Aba.'

The old woman looked steadily at the back of Sister Ria's veil. 'It is not important. He is the Patrón,' she said firmly.

Sister Ria shook her head. 'It is important. To me.'

They stood for a while without speaking, the old woman watching the young nun, Sister Ria gazing blindly out the window at the dark land.

Finally, she said, 'My sister Milagros?'

'She was written to. She has not come.' There was a cold sound to the words.

'You never cared for Milagros.'

The old woman waited a moment before she said, 'Were you taught rudeness at this convent, or is it just your nature?'

'She will come,' Sister Ria said softly. 'In the meantime, there are things we must do. The Chinese boy?'

'Min.'

As soon as Aba had spoken his name, the young man stepped forward out of a nearby doorway where he had been quietly waiting, and Sister Ria jumped at the sight of him. Min grinned and then bowed, remaining bent over.

'Stand up, please. You should not bow to me.'

Aba shot her a stern look but Sister Ria ignored her.

The boy straightened, the grin still cutting his face in half, and slipped his hands into the long sleeves of his gown of yellow Chinese silk. He had tied a matching ribbon smartly in his pigtail.

'I have told Min to remove the animals and to have Father's room cleaned.'

'The Patrón will not allow it,' Aba said.

Sister Ria ignored the comment. 'Do we have carbolic acid?' she asked, sounding once more the convent nurse. 'If we do, have the servants use it on the floors. And the curtains in the Patrón's room must be taken down so sunlight can be let in.' She waited a moment, then went on, 'And no more animals or opium are to be taken to his room.'

'He will allow none of this.'

'He is not well and these things must be done,' Sister Ria spoke in the tone she had often used to urge reluc-

24

tant labourers to accomplish tasks at the poor convent hospital.

'We are not the Patrón.'

'For the Patrón's own good.'

Aba thought about this for a moment. 'Perhaps I will attempt these things, Isadora,' she said, 'but only if you show him proper respect.'

Sister Ria smiled at the old woman. Aba had always stood between her and her father, balancing the imbalance of their two lives. Sister Ria loved her for many things; she loved her for that. 'Yes,' she said, 'the respect he deserves.'

Aba caught the tone. 'Isadora, do not play games with me. You are no longer a child.'

Sister Ria clasped her hands at the waist and nodded.

They had been standing in the hallway for close to an hour, Aba waiting patiently, as she had waited on Sister Ria's mother, then after her mother's death on the oldest daughter, Milagros. Sister Ria turned and looked back out the window at the last of evening.

'I'm tired, Aba.'

The woman tipped her head and began walking down the loggia in her brisk stride. With her slower steps Sister Ria quickly fell behind, and though she tried to resist she glanced around her. The convent rule of modesty of the eyes seemed pointless in this house.

She stopped in front of a beautiful oil painting in a magnificent golden frame. Candles in wall sconces burned on both sides of it, casting soft light over the lovely scene. Her father had painted it the year she left – an old woman watching a passing throng of sheep and goats, herd dogs and sun-weathered shepherds moving down a summer road. The old woman in the scene was not Aba, he had never painted Aba. Aba had been the head servant at La Cienega for more than forty years – her father painting for hours every day, using maids and field hands by the dozen as models in his work – but she had never seen him paint Aba.

Sister Ria swallowed hard and looked down at the floor. And except for one time – a time she still did not understand – he had never painted her either. She squeezed her hands together until they hurt. She had to stop thinking these things, she hadn't come back to pity herself. She had come because of her mother. Nothing more, nothing less.

Her eyes returned to the painting. It was lovely. She could almost hear the sounds and see the movement in the still liquid of the canvas. In his youth, her father had studied in Paris and Rome. He was an accomplished artist, there was no refuting that. But that was the only testament she could make on his behalf.

Aba had stopped walking and stood looking back at her, frowning. The old woman tapped her stick twice on the floor, the noise echoing against the walls. Sister Ria jumped at the sound and pulled her clasped hands tighter into her waist and looked down at the floor. 'I'm sorry, Aba,' she said, knowing the old woman hated idleness.

Aba watched her a moment longer and then shook her head and asked, 'Have you forgotten all that I taught?'

'No.'

'Then when you talk to me – look at me. And speak up. You are the daughter of the Patrón.'

Sister Ria raised her head. 'Everything is fine, Aba.'

'No, it is not. But it will become so.'

Sister Ria did not sleep in her bedroom that night. Instead, she took a heavy blue comforter and returned to the hallway in front of her father's room, pulled a large leather wing chair directly opposite his door, and sat. She dozed off and on throughout the night into the early morning hours, as if keeping a death vigil, only fully awakening when Aba brought her a tray of coffee and small sweet cakes. The old woman remained standing nearby watching her holding the cup in both hands, sipping the liquid through a cloud of steam. Sister Ria ignored the servant and peered through the rising vapours of her coffee at the heavy door to Don Maximiato's room, as if determined to will the old man to come out and face her.

'This is not right, child. Go to your bedroom before the other servants see you. It is unseemly.'

Sister Ria shook her head no.

'He will not do as you wish.'

'Then he will have no peace.'

It was the old woman's turn to shake her head. Then she stopped, remembering her position, bowed stiffly and said, 'Is there anything you need?'

'No thank you.'

Aba nodded and walked away down the long hallway.

'I love you,' Sister Ria called after her.

If she heard, Aba did not respond.

The head servant had obviously told the other servants to stay out of the main hallway of the house, since the time on the nearby pendulum clock read 12.10 in the afternoon and none of the house workers had appeared. Then Sister Ria heard the heavy metal lock on the bedroom door turn. A small crack appeared and through it she glimpsed a narrow strip of her father's face peering out at her. She sat up straighter. Hurriedly Don Maximiato closed the door and locked it again. Sister Ria said nothing.

When Aba came down the hallway an hour later, she was followed by the Chinese boy, Min, who carried a heavy tray of food and drink. Aba bowed her head politely at Sister Ria and unlocked the door to the Patrón's bedroom, letting Min enter. Then the old servant turned and stood outside the door, her arms crossed over her thin chest, ignoring Sister Ria.

'I will not force my way into the room,' Sister Ria said.

Aba said nothing.

Min came out of the room minutes later, carrying a pottery waste jar. He bowed at Sister Ria and then he and Aba marched off down the hallway leaving Sister Ria to her silent watch. Twice that afternoon, Min delivered food and drink to her. On his second trip, the boy stood looking at her sympathetically, but he was too well trained to speak to the Patrón's daughter of personal matters.

'I am fine,' she said, as if reading his mind.

He smiled and started to bow.

'No, please –'

He stood and grinned and walked off down the hall.

Periodically throughout the afternoon, Aba would step out into the hallway from a distance and check to see that she was still there. Each time, the old servant would shake her head and then retreat. Tiring of the chair, Sister Ria began to pace back and forth in front of the door, and twice she made a quick trip to the new water closet that had been installed down the hallway. The house was silent and she felt alone – sensations that she had lived with for the past eight years. She would outlast him, she told herself.

He could not stay locked in his room much longer. He simply did not have the patience for it. He hated restraint of any kind. His life, she knew, was an odd whipsawing

28

of irrational whims and impulses. No, he could not last inside his bedroom for very long. And when he came out, she would ask him again if he had murdered the woman. If he said yes, there would be nothing she could do for him, beyond prayer.

Don Maximiato restrained himself throughout the evening. And to her surprise, he failed to appear that night and through the next day. To her greater surprise, her own patience was badly stretched and she began to pace in front of his door in a very unchristian way.

'You have behaved like this all of your life,' she said through the thick wooden door. 'It worked when I was a child. But I am no longer a child and it will no longer work. Do you hear?'

She put an ear to the door and listened. No sound.

'I know you are in there.'

Nothing.

'I am not going away.'

Silence.

She brought her hands, palms together, to her face. 'And you will not anger me. Do you hear that as well?'

If he did, he did not reply.

The hours began to pass more slowly. She continued to pace, reciting the rosary, the Nicene Creed, the Lord's Prayer, the Twenty-third Psalm. Not until the middle of the following day did he finally emerge. She was certain that he must have a spy-hole somewhere in the wall or door of his room since he caught her completely by surprise as she sat in the water closet. She heard the great door opening on its heavy iron hinges and small footsteps sneaking quickly down the hallway.

'You wait right there,' she said through a narrow crack in the bathroom door.

He did not wait.

'I want to talk to you,' she called, rushing to get her habit on straight.

She caught up with Don Maximiato as he was heading through the library's large French doors that opened out into the hacienda's lovely rose garden. He was dressed in a beautiful green caftan and moving fast. She pressed her lips together and marched after him down a narrow brick pathway edged on both sides by deep green foliage, then through a large red gate set in a great tawny brown mud wall. She pulled the gate shut behind her so that he could not escape and turned around. It was if she had been transported to Morocco. The enclosure behind the gate was covered with a floor of sand; a tent of black camel hair stood in the centre, surrounded by palms and olive trees. The only thing missing, she thought, was a small herd of goats. She shook her head at his play-acting.

'Father, we need to talk.'

The Patrón paid no attention to her. He sat on a small stool and took off his sandals and then washed his face at a stone fountain and his feet in a tiled tank sunk in the sand. Not once did he look in her direction, as if oblivious to the fact that she was standing only a few feet away. Then he spread a small blue and red carpet on the sand in front of the tent and knelt and closed his eyes in meditation. She was directly in front of him, standing with her hands on her hips.

'Father,' she said, 'stop what you are doing and listen. I need to –' She hesitated. He was obviously at his midday prayers. The shame of interrupting a man at prayer caused her to step back and stop talking. He opened one eye and looked at her.

'You should be veiled,' he said.

30

'I'm not a Muslim.'

'You should be veiled,' he repeated.

'I'm not a Muslim,' she said again, slowly for emphasis.

'You should be veil –'

'Enough! Please.'

There was the hint of a satisfied smile on his face, his lips pressed together so that he looked like a lizard that had just swallowed a fly. He shut his eye.

She studied him closely: the remains of a decent-looking face, a high thin nose, hair gone thin and white, his cheeks sunken. He looked tired, his body far thinner than she had remembered. He was speaking Arabic now. She waited out of respect for God, not him.

When he had finished, Don Maximiato stood and shook the small rug and began to roll it into a neat tube. Sister Ria inched closer like a panther about to pounce. She opened her mouth and then quickly shut it. She had rehearsed this moment every day for the past two months, how she would do this and say that, but now that it was here all she could do was open and shut her mouth like a wooden puppet.

Suddenly, he stopped rolling the carpet and looked up and said, 'May I help you?'

She clasped her hands at her waist and nodded.

He grew suddenly impatient. 'If you have something to say, please say it.'

'I have tried to forgive you,' she blurted, 'but I cannot.'

He shrugged. 'I don't need it.'

'I need it,' she snapped.

'Adding up your little hurts?'

'They are not little hurts!'

'I thought you had come to ask if I was a murderer,' Don Maximiato said, dancing a playful jig in the sand

31

and then turning and walking out the gate and back up the narrow garden path to the house. Sister Ria trailed behind him, her face red with rage.

'It has taken me years to be able to do this,' she said as they moved down the long hallway. 'You cannot just walk off as if nothing happened. Do you understand?'

Don Maximiato yawned and kept walking.

When they were halfway down the hall from his bedroom, Don Maximiato suddenly broke into a sprint, Sister Ria bolting after him. The old man feinted left into a nearby corridor and Sister Ria took the fake and turned off. Immediately, she whirled around and rushed back into the loggia and saw Don Maximiato walking calmly into his bedroom.

She stomped in after him. 'You will not walk off!'

'Isadora.'

Sister Ria stood opening and clenching her hands, glaring at her father as he crawled up onto his bed, then she turned and faced Aba.

'Come here, child,' the old servant said.

The old man fluffed his pillows, then picked up his sketch pad and pencil and leaned back and began to draw.

Sister Ria turned back to him, collecting herself before she said, 'I loved you and you sliced my heart out.' She studied his face for a long time. 'But you are right. I have come because I promised Mother I would come. And so I ask you again, did you kill that woman?'

He said nothing.

'Isadora,' the old woman repeated, 'come out of the room.'

'I will wait for your answer. I swear.'

He stuck his tongue out at her.

In response, she tipped a basket of peaches sitting on

32

the table onto the floor, the fruit rolling in every direction, and walked out.

Sister Ria once again refused to leave the hallway in front of her father's bedroom, taking up her position in the large leather chair while Aba stood and watched her. They said nothing to one another. Sister Ria was shamefully aware that she had sunk to his childish level in her attempt to force him to tell her the truth. But surely God understood.

Sister Ria was not certain when she had fallen asleep or when she had been taken to her room. The exhaustion of two months of difficult travelling, little food and less sleep had finally taken its full toll. She sat up in her bed and looked around her. Her room had not changed. It was as if she had just stepped out into the hallway for a moment and returned. Her childhood clothes still hung in the French armoire, her mirror and brushes still lay on her dressing table. Aba had dressed her in her nightgown and opened the door to the central garden.

She breathed in deeply of the smell of roses, her eyes moving over the things of her past, slowly transported by memory back some fifteen years to the time when her only name was Isadora.

It was a warm summer morning, one week after the deaths of her mother and brother from smallpox. She was ten years old and standing in this same room with its thick adobe walls and the window stuffed with pillows where she often played with her dolls or daydreamed. The window opened out onto the lovely courtyard garden of bougainvillaea, orange and lemon trees and roses. Roses were everywhere. They were her father's favourite. The beds overflowed with them, with their magnificent range

33

of colour – yellow, orange, peach, red – and delicious fragrance.

On this morning, she was surrounded by three or four of the Indian and Mexican women who worked in the house. They were quietly caring for her. The room was damp with the warm smell of perfume and bath water. Aba, who had been the hacienda's head servant since before Isadora's birth, was combing her long dark hair while the others dressed her in a beautiful white dress of satin that her mother had bought for her the year before. Then suddenly her father was there, yelling and cursing and driving the women out of the room. Only Aba remained, standing loyally, defiantly in front of her.

'You will no longer dress her like a girl,' he said. 'You may dress her sister in that manner, but not this child.'

Her father was not a large man, he was thin and shorter in height than Aba, but in his rage he seemed a giant to Isadora.

'She is a girl, Don Maximiato,' Aba said. 'Soon to be a young lady. She needs to begin to dress like one.' Her voice was firm.

'Do not lecture me, woman. You will not pamper this child. She will not wear dresses.'

'There is a mass this afternoon for Ramón, Father,' Isadora said.

'There is no mass and you will not speak of Ramón again. Put on your riding pants and blouse.'

Aba was still standing between them. Trembling, Isadora took a step to the side. It was the first time in her life she had tried to defy him.

'There is a mass. And I must go.'

'No.' He turned and faced the servant. 'And you will shave her hair.'

'It is not right,' Aba said.

'I did not ask you, woman.'

Aba did not move.

'You will do these things!' he shouted.

Sister Ria refused to cry. She lay back on her pillows and tried to forget. From the angle of the moonlight in the open doorway, she knew that it was well past midnight. Moist air drifting in from the garden carried the smell of plant growth and she could see the ancient stone pergola and behind it the beautiful terraced walls. But her thoughts were not on the moonlight or the garden.

She rolled onto her side and prayed for forgiveness for the corruption of her soul, squeezing her hands together until they hurt. Then the familiar sense of bitterness rose in her like an ocean tide. 'Forgive me, I don't know how to stop hating him. I have tried, Lord. I've tried.' For the past eight years she had hidden her hatred for him beneath the never-ending hours spent nursing the sick and dying. But two months ago, when she had received the letter about the murder and the charges against him, the hatred in her had begun to stir to life like an insect that had lain dormant for years in its cocoon.

She pounded her hand on the pillow. 'I don't know how to stop hating him!' She knew only that as a Sister of Mercy she had a sacred responsibility to Christ: To be at peace, to have tender mercy for others, to forgive – she felt her muscles tensing – to honour her father.

And she had failed.

And God knew.

She fought the trembling in her body and looked around her in growing desperation. The house was silent. 'Lord. Please,' she sobbed, 'I don't know how.' She calmed herself and listened to the night wind until the old cat jumped silently up onto the end of the bed, sitting arrogantly with his back to her. Thankful for the distraction, she wiped the dampness from her face on the sheets and smiled. 'There you are. Shame on you for scratching poor Aba. Until you learn to behave, I'm calling you Fern.' She narrowed her eyes at the old tom. 'Do you hear me?'

Fernando looked at her with an expression that said he was more annoyed that she was talking to him than by whatever she chose to call him. She could see that his eye socket had been flushed and salved and the dried dirt and blood washed from his fur. Around his neck was tied a poultice of some sort. Sister Ria felt a surge of love for the old servant.

Fernando was turning back to the shadows when Sister Ria heard something scrape on the tile floor and knew that someone or something else besides the cat was in the darkness with her. She opened her mouth slightly so that her breathing would not interfere with her hearing, and listened for another sound, her eyes probing the layers of night surrounding the bed. Nothing. Then she saw a dark human-like shape in a corner of the room.

'Aba?'

Silence.

'Is that you?'

There was no response.

'Father?'

The only answer was a sharp metallic sound, a hard snap of metal that seemed to trigger an explosion of noise and movement in the darkness: something alive and maniacal was rushing back and forth in the shadows, banging into furniture.

Then the room fell silent and she probed the shadows with her eyes. The figure was gone. She was taking small bites of air as if she couldn't catch her breath and shaking hard, a familiar odour drifting in the air. She waited. Moments later, she heard footsteps outside in the garden, then the closing of a door.

She continued to wait.

Nothing moved. When she could no longer bear the waiting, she lit the candle on the nightstand, the light tossing distorted shadows against the walls. Her breath caught in her throat. Slowly she crossed the floor and held the candle closer to the wall, then backed away. Someone had smeared a rough Latin cross in blood on the plaster. She could not take her eyes off it, as if God himself had made the mark against her.

Suddenly there was movement on the floor again and she jumped back and quickly raised the candle, casting a larger circle of light over the room. Blood was everywhere. The small head was lying in a corner, the eyes gazing dully into the shadows. The lifeless body lay in another corner, the dead rooster's wings still rising and falling slowly. Fernando was sitting close by it, watching intently the poor headless creature's last movements. Then one of the bird's legs stretched out, the claws closing as if trying to grasp the old cat. Fernando hopped away. The body was still now.

Sister Ria crossed herself, then, clutching her crucifix, she unlocked her bedroom door and walked quickly out into the long darkened hallway, stopping and listening, her eyes probing the gloom for the intruder. Nothing. There was a black emptiness between the massive adobe walls of the wide hallway. The only sound was the soft ticking of a clock. She saw that it was 2.00 a.m. Sister Ria crept forward and the old cat did the same, moving like a small leopard on the prowl, making a strange gnashing sound with his teeth. She was glad he was with her.

Twenty minutes later she had searched the library, the huge kitchen, the receiving room, closets and storage pantries and other likely hiding places and had found no one. Then the realization struck her: there was no intruder. It must have been her father. He had killed the rooster and smeared the vile cross on the wall to frighten her.

Sister Ria pounded on the locked door of his room until her hands hurt. But he neither answered the door nor spoke. She stopped pounding and stood rubbing her hands together, leaning in close and listening. There was no sound. But she was certain he was inside, mocking her.

'You ruined my life,' she shouted. 'But you will not frighten me! Do you understand?'

She had turned and was starting back down the hallway to her bedroom when suddenly a shadow moved. She whirled and faced it and watched as Aba stepped into a shaft of pale moonlight that spilled into the loggia, the glow giving the old woman an ethereal look.

'Nina?' Aba asked her. 'What is the trouble?'

'Father was in my room,' she said, rushing her words. She tried to calm herself, continuing more slowly, 'He killed a gallo . . . then fled into the garden, then back into the house.'

Aba was still dressed. She was drying her hands on a small towel.

'Father killed a rooster –'

'No, he did not. He was not in your room. He did not kill a rooster.'

'Aba, there is blood everywhere. He killed a rooster –'

'There are *ladrones* – thieves.'

'It wasn't a thief.' Sister Ria paused, trying to make

38

sense of what had just happened. 'Why would a thief kill something in my room?'

'Perhaps to frighten you away.'

'It wasn't a thief.'

'Los ladrones,' Aba said, as if she hadn't heard, 'believe that since the Patrón is to be executed he has hidden his gold in the walls of the hacienda.'

The woman had begun walking down the darkened hallway towards Sister Ria's room. Sister Ria stared at the back of her head, waiting until she found her voice again. 'What did you say?'

'That the thieves –'

'No – that he is to be executed.'

The old servant turned and stood looking at her.

'Aba?'

'In eight days.'

FOUR

The night had seemed endless. Sister Ria was pacing back and forth in front of the Patrón's bedroom and listening to the familiar *vit-vit-vit* of the little *golondrinas* – swallows – building their mud nesting cups under the eaves of the hacienda, the graceful little birds skimming water in flight from the large fountain near the front veranda.

She had been sick twice during the night.

Aba leaned against a wall of the loggia and watched her. The old woman was framed in a patch of bright sunlight and looked as if she was finally in one of the Patrón's paintings. 'He does not deserve this, Isadora,' she snapped.

'I am doing nothing to him.'

'You are stalking back and forth in front of his room.'

'I'm waiting, that's all.'

'He doesn't deserve it.'

Sister Ria looked at the woman, overcome by emotions that swirled in her like a kaleidoscope. 'And what does he deserve, Aba?'

Aba pushed away from the wall, too quickly for the

movement to be perceived as anything but angry, and started to answer, then stopped.

'No,' Sister Ria said, 'forget that you are the head servant. Say whatever you wish. You believe he deserves better, Aba. Tell me what he deserves. Because I don't know.'

Aba shook her head.

'Tell me.'

When Aba spoke, the sound was almost inaudible. 'Peace,' was all she said. The woman began to retreat slowly down the hallway. She looked broken.

'Aba.'

The servant stopped and raised her chin, her back to Sister Ria.

Sister Ria cleared her throat and in a firm voice said, 'He deserves peace.'

Aba nodded and walked down the hall.

Sister Ria watched until the woman disappeared around a turn and then wrapped her arms around her shoulders as if she were hugging herself. She stood trying to answer the nagging questions that surged like seawater through her brain. She had no answers. None. All she had was her promise to her mother, and the fact that her father was going to die and she could not stop hating him.

It was a dark staining sin.

Sister Ria was kneeling in the hallway in front of his room, praying for both their souls, when the door opened and the Patrón walked out dressed as an Englishman: black frock-coat, towering top hat and cane, looking like an undertaker. In another time and place, she might have laughed. But not now. This time was horribly different.

'Good morning, Father,' she said quietly, then stood and

stepped to the side to let him pass. 'Is there anything I can do for you?'

The Patrón touched the cane to the brim of his hat and said nothing, as if he had never before laid eyes on her, as if she were a complete stranger of no special worth in his privileged world. Instantly, as if she had been yanked backwards in time, she felt like a child again. He moved past her and down the hallway.

The old familiar frustration rose in her breast and she whispered, 'Damn you.' Then in a louder voice she called after him: 'You don't even know who I am. Worse, you don't care!' She stood wringing her hands and then she yelled, 'I am your daughter – say it!'

He did not.

Fernando was sitting in the centre of the loggia, watching her with an expression that said that, like Aba, he also disapproved of her behaviour. 'I know,' she muttered, 'I know.' The old cat ignored her and licked his paws. She reached down to scratch his head and he took a wild bolo punch of a haymaker at her. She walked after her father.

He was sitting in the garden on a bench, looking perfectly relaxed as if he had not a care in this life. She sat on a bench opposite him and collected herself. When she had calmed sufficiently, she said, 'I apologize, Father.' Realizing that he would be dead in eight days, Sister Ria began to look at him differently. The sense of mistrust and loathing were still there inside her, but there was something else, something she couldn't identify, something that made her study the lines of his face, his hands, to watch his breathing, the rise and fall of his narrow chest, the movement of his eyes.

He was wearing a strange assortment of her mother's jewellery pinned to the frock-coat in various places, looking like some oddly decorated old soldier of the tsars. Suddenly, for no apparent reason, he began poking the cane in the air, as if fencing with a phantom.

'It's a lovely morning, Father.'

He hacked harder at the air.

'How are you feeling?'

He turned on the bench so that he was no longer facing her and continued his mad thrusts at vital parts of the firmament. Sister Ria straightened the folds of her habit and tried to think of something that might interest him. But all she could think of were the indignities of her life at the hands of this man.

As quickly as it had started, the Patrón's mad assault on the heavens ceased and he began feeding his pet peacock, Sari, handfuls of grain pulled from the pocket of his frock-coat, holding the kernels in his palm and letting the large green bird peck at them. Fernando was interested in this development and he hopped up on the bench next to Sister Ria and sat watching the enormous creature in wonder, his fur rising over his body and a strange rasping sound escaping from his throat.

'You shouldn't be hunting birds,' she told him.

The old cat paid no attention, his one eye glued on the peacock. Moments later, having settled on a strategy, he hopped down and began to slink towards the massive bird.

'Don't you dare,' she snapped. The cat froze and flattened himself on the ground, his tail twitching back and forth like a lion's.

'Here, kitty, kitty,' Don Maximiato chuckled, 'get the birdie.'

'Please don't encourage him.'

The old man dusted his hands of the grain then put his thumbs in his ears and fanned his fingers at her and fluttered his tongue. Sister Ria ignored him. Fernando ignored them both and was starting to slink over the ground again, when Sari decided he'd had enough of the foolish tomcat. He flared his gigantic tail-feathers, dropped his wings and scurried at the cat.

That was a mistake. While ten times Fernando's size, the bird had none of his speed and quickness, and Fernando was on his back in a flash, raking feathers from the poor creature at an alarming rate. He was just about to bite the back of Sari's neck when Sister Ria grabbed for him. The wily cat saw her coming and bolted off the bird into the garden. The Patrón was howling with laughter and stomping his feet.

Sister Ria sat back down and watched him, slowly shaking her head. He was as childish and erratic as ever. She took a deep breath, 'I told myself I was the reason for the way you treated me.' She blew the air out of her lungs. 'But I wasn't. I –'

Her father interrupted her with a ditty sung in falsetto. Knowing his little ballads were mostly bawdy tales about the anatomy of women, she turned and started back towards the house, humming 'Amazing Grace'.

She had refused supper and was lying under the covers of her bed, propped against the pillows contemplating the open armoire in front of her. She could see her waist-coats, the velvet and satin dress pants, the tall leather riding boots, the sombreros . . . all of it the fashion of a young Mexican male. She closed her eyes tight against the memories.

Aba was sitting on a wooden chair just inside the doorway of the room, waiting silently on Sister Ria. The old woman had not moved or spoken in quite a while and Sister Ria jumped when she said, 'Eight days.'

Sister Ria stared at her, opening her eyes wide and arching her eyebrows, waiting for her to continue. She did not.

'There is nothing I can do,' Sister Ria said.

Aba did not change her expression.

'Nothing.'

'When I first saw you, Isadora, I thought you had come to save him.'

'No.'

Aba gazed at the floor. 'You were always compassionate as a child – begging me to give food and money to the poor. Now you are a nun – but have no compassion. How is that, child?'

'Aba, listen to me.'

The old servant looked up at her.

'If he won't tell me whether or not he murdered that woman, there is nothing I can do for him.'

Aba continued to watch her. 'Nothing you will do, you mean.' Then she stood and left the room, pulling the door closed behind her.

'Wait,' Sister Ria called.

She hopped down from her bed and went out into the hallway. The servant was at the far end.

'Aba –' Sister Ria called.

The woman continued walking.

It was almost dawn, and Sister Ria was holding her breath when the old servant answered her knock and opened the door to her small room at the rear of the hacienda. Aba was still dressed. She looked tired.

'Yes, child?'

Sister Ria just stared at her.

'Isadora?'

Sister Ria studied the lines of the old face for a time before she said, 'I'll look into it.'

SEVEN DAYS . . .

FIVE

Sister Ria gazed intently at the photograph of the young woman. She had been thinking about Dorothy Regal for so long, she felt she knew her. But the face of the girl in the picture looked different from the face Sister Ria had created in her mind, younger, more vulnerable. The girl was naked and child-awkward, lying on her back on the floor of a small room. Her throat had been cut. Her face was hard with death.

Sister Ria had seen the torn and decaying corpses of hundreds of young women – dead from childbirth, disease and violence. She had prepared their bodies for burial and prayed over their souls. She had dressed them in their finest garments, and when they had nothing decent she had begged clothing for them. She was familiar with the dead of her sex. Still, her breath came in short gasps and she pressed her lips together as if trying to hold back a scream.

The voice of the man sitting across the desk from her brought Sister Ria back. 'The night watchman found her, the way you see her.' He paused before he continued, 'She was carrying a child. The foetus was removed from her. We never found it.'

'Who was she?' Sister Ria asked, not liking the impatient tone of the man's voice.

'Prostitute.'

'Yes, but where did she come from? Did she have family? Other children that need taking care of?'

'Wasn't from here.' He pointed a finger at the photograph. 'Handprints on her shoulders,' he said as if it mattered. 'Whoever cut her throat held her down while she bled to death.'

Sister Ria gently touched her fingers to the gaping wound in Dorothy Regal's belly, then drew an invisible cross over the stomach of the girl and another over Dorothy Regal's forehead and in a weak voice said, 'She's naked.'

'Prostitute,' he repeated, as if this made her nakedness acceptable.

She turned the photograph over, raising her eyes until she was looking over her reading glasses into the face of Raymond Hood, Los Angeles City's police chief. From another photograph in a wooden frame on his desk it appeared that he had a staff of fifteen policemen. She remembered when the town had had nothing more than an old Mexican who served part time as sheriff – with a borrowed pistol – and part time as carpenter. 'She is naked,' Sister Ria repeated, firmly.

Hood was middle-aged, balding some, with a long thin and deeply tanned face. He studied the features of this beautiful young nun – her face made all the more appealing, almost picture-like, by the perfect white headband framing it. Having watched her walk into his office, he knew that beneath the shapeless habit her body was strong – tall and slender, with a nice way of moving – and the thought

50

crossed his mind that a nunnery was a waste of her. He pushed himself up from his chair and stepped to a wooden filing cabinet and took out a yellow envelope. Sister Ria handed the photograph to him. 'Thank you,' she said and took off her glasses.

The room smelled of gun oil and burnt powder and she figured there was a firing range somewhere in the building.

'And my father had been with her?'

'We never found anyone who saw your father that night.' By the light of the hurricane lamp on the desk, the man's eyes were tired looking. 'No witnesses. Nobody heard anything,' he told her, flipping through a stack of papers on his desk as if signalling that he had other more important work waiting.

'Then I don't understand.'

Hood put the papers down and placed a large cardboard box on the desk. 'We found these things in her room.' He removed a black gaucho hat and a leather belt with a large gold buckle, and set them on the desk. Sister Ria was fighting her sense of dislike of the man's arrogance.

'Those are common —'

'Not with your father's initials stamped on them.'

Sister Ria put her tiny spectacles back on and peered inside at the hatband. The letters MRL were clearly visible in the leather. Maximiato Rialto Lugo. She pulled off her glasses and rubbed her eyes.

'Did he confess? Make any statement?'

'No.'

'Did he even know Dorothy Regal?'

Hood blew his nose in a handkerchief. 'The woman rented her room from the Fiesta — she wasn't one of their girls.'

51

She could feel her temper heating at the coldness of the man. 'Meaning?'

'Meaning we don't know who her clients were. But we have your father's things – so he was one of them.'

'You figure, but you don't know.'

'We have his things.'

'Things that could have been placed there by anyone.'

The man looked annoyed. 'We have his things,' he repeated.

'What else, Mr Hood?'

'Nothing.'

With the finality of that pronouncement still ringing in the air, Fernando, who had accompanied her in the wagon that morning, leapt agilely up onto Chief Hood's desk, sniffed a pile of official-looking papers, then curled up in a nicely tucked ball in the centre of the ink blotter. The police chief, clearly not used to having feral cats turn his desk into a bed, looked annoyed.

'That animal looks like he could carry the ringworm.'

'Just hurt,' Sister Ria said.

Fernando yawned.

'He doesn't look to be in much pain to me, ma'am. What's his name?' There was no interest or affection in the question – more a practical matter, as if he might be collecting information for an arrest report.

'Fern.'

The man raised his eyebrows slightly. 'It's a male cat, Miss Lugo.'

'Yes. But he's being punished.'

The chief looked at her as if she might be a little touched in the head, then reached both hands to pick up the tom.

'I wouldn't do that,' she said. 'He isn't friendly.'

The man stopped and sized up the mangy-looking animal

slumbering arrogantly in the centre of his desk. He was a very big, very ugly cat, with scars over most of his body. The chief pursed his lips, then he seemed to have a brand-new thought and slowly began to put the evidence items back into the cardboard box. Fernando was purring, the sound like a coarse file over iron.

Sister Ria gazed at the police chief's bow tie, her thoughts drifting.

She had driven into town that morning on the old dirt road that cut through the vineyard and fields, the look of things so familiar that the years of her absence had seemed to recede into the far distance. She had caught herself noticing small details – whether the tomatoes had been staked up to keep the fruit from rotting on the earth, whether the spring growth in the vineyard had been properly tied on the Guyot supports.

It had been her job to know these things.

He had made it her job.

She had stopped at the side of the road and cautioned a group of young peones working the wooden irrigation gates that controlled the flow of river water down the rows of guero chillis that too much water would sweeten the crop, damaging it. Not certain they had understood, she had crawled down from her carriage and pulled the heavy wooden gate up, the muddy water flowing over her shoes and the hem of her robe. She had waded through the thick liquid and yanked other gates up to show them exactly how much water to let into the furrows.

The young men were stunned at the sight of a woman, a nun no less, trudging around in the mud and water, muscling the irrigation gates, and instructing them in the proper watering of chilli plants. But it was second nature to her. After the death of her brother Ramón she had been

53

painstakingly taught to manage the vast lands and herds of La Cienega. And she would never be the same.

Chief Hood was drumming his fingers impatiently on the desktop.

She focused on the man. 'Nobody knows whether my father even knew this woman. And there are no witnesses . . . just his hat and belt?'

Hood removed a sharp-bladed carving knife from the box and laid it down in front of her. Sister Ria saw the Lugo family crest on the heavy silver handle. 'On the floor next to the body.'

She stared at the blade of the knife until the police chief said, 'Anything else, Miss Lugo?'

'You've left him at home.'

Fernando had risen from his brief nap and was stretching lazily in the centre of the desk. Hood had his eyes on him. 'Mexicans think your father is some sort of god,' he said, watching the large tom. 'I don't need trouble with them. And something tells me he's not the running type.'

Hood made a quick move to shove Fernando off the desk. But it wasn't quick enough and Fernando sank his fangs into the police chief's hand and then sprang out the door.

Sister Ria stood and straightened her habit. 'That's why he is being called Fern, sir.' Hood was sucking on his hand. She wanted to kiss the old cat but figured it would be dangerous.

Sister Ria stood at the bottom of the jailhouse stairs, trying to think clearly and shivering in the hot morning air. All her life she had prided herself on being able to get her mind to work straight during times of trouble, but this time was different. Too much of her life was tied to this time. She pulled her shawl over her shoulders and gazed at the heavy three-storeyed brick jail, squinting against the sunshine.

The building stood in the centre of a large barren lot on the north-west corner of Spring and Jail streets, a squat imposing structure so very serious and different looking from the little converted adobe chicken coop that had served that same purpose when she was a girl. So much had changed.

She turned and walked down the brick path to the side-walk, leaving the jail and the American business district behind her. Fernando trotted after her, meowing loudly about the fact that he had to walk all over town. 'I didn't ask you to come along,' she said, 'but thank you for what you did in there.' The old tom looked up at her and seemed to realize he wasn't going to persuade her and quit wasting his breath.

She entered La Calle de los Mercados – Market Road – a wide dirt street lined on one side by sun-washed white adobe walls splashed over by pink and white sprays of wistaria and on the other by small shops open to the front.

People were moving through the little stores and Mexican boys were scurrying in and out carrying trays of steaming coffee, hot chocolate and fruit juices to their customers. When she had lived here, this had been the only place to shop. She let her gaze drift over the powdery marketplace, finding it easy and comforting to imagine herself a girl again, the town a small pueblo, her mother and brother still alive, her father not sentenced to death. She tensed at this last thought, balling her hands into fists until they began to throb.

I don't know what to do, Mother.

She shrugged off her sense of hopelessness and continued

walking, the vendors beckoning her. There was an old toothless Mexican woman sitting in the shade of a pastry stall being fanned by a small Indian girl of six or seven. The child was barely able to pull the long rope that worked a complicated series of pulleys causing the large canvas fan to wave back and forth over the pastries and the old woman who sat drinking coffee from a small porcelain cup held daintily between her gnarled thumb and forefinger.

When Sister Ria stopped to look at the child, the woman motioned to her with a welcoming sweep of her hand over the mounds of food. 'Sister of God, come inside my humble stall, please.' The old woman grinned a toothless smile, covering her mouth with a withered hand. 'These are heavenly dulces.'

Sister Ria ignored her and her pastries and stepped closer to the child. 'Have you had a meal this morning?' she asked in Spanish. The girl in her tattered dress reminded her of the orphans who wandered the streets and alleys of Poona, and the hollow sensation she always felt for them clutched like a hand at her throat.

Her thoughts turned to her Sisters in India and she smiled sadly. She had convinced them that – tired as they were – God wanted them to care for the orphans as well as the lepers. And when they were not working in the hospital, they would leave the village and beg food and money for the lost children of Poona.

'Have you eaten?' she asked the little girl.

The child stopped pulling on the rope and looked up at her and shook her head, the eyes burning into Sister Ria. The old woman stomped her foot and the little girl jumped and started pulling on the rope again. Sister Ria took the rope from her hand and gave the little girl a coin from the small bag of coins Aba had left for her on her nightstand. 'Go and have breakfast.'

The girl hung back, nervously clutching the coin and staring at the old hag.

'Blessed Sister –' the old woman said, 'you have no right –'

Sister Ria leaned forward and placed a second coin into the woman's outstretched hand.

'But for this,' the woman said, her eyes brightening, 'she can take time for a meal.' She waved the child away, lest Sister Ria take back her coin. The girl ran.

'She's a child, she should not be worked like a beast of burden,' Sister Ria said, pulling on the rope to keep the fan waving and the flies off the pastries.

'It is how she lives. I care for her.'

'I can see that,' Sister Ria snapped, in no mood to be trifled with. Then she stopped herself and took a deep breath, reciting silently her vows to offer only tender mercy to others. She calmed down and said, 'She is too small for the task.'

The old woman shrugged. 'Perhaps, but it is all that I have for her.'

Sister Ria handed the rope to the woman and started to move away but the old merchant clutched at her hand and moaned, 'Sister, bless me with a prayer, for I am very old.'

Sister Ria hesitated. 'If you promise God to treat the child better.'

The woman nodded and Sister Ria put her hand on the thin head and said, 'Lord, bless this woman who has committed to you with her whole heart to take better care of this child – bless her with a long and healthy life.' Then the firm tones of a convent nurse returned to her voice,

'But only if she does as she has promised, Lord.'

The old hag frowned at Sister Ria, who stood looking down at her for a moment before she said, 'You must do what you have promised God. Do you understand?' The woman sneered. Sister Ria raised her eyebrows. Reluctantly, the old woman nodded and Sister Ria made the sign of the cross on the mottled skin of her forehead.

She had started walking through the small stalls of the marketplace again, when she heard the old woman mutter a curse behind her. She stopped and looked back at the woman. 'God will check to see that you are caring for the child.' The old crone frowned and Sister Ria said, 'I have asked God to send an angel to watch you, to see that you keep your promise to our Lord.'

The old woman's mouth dropped open and she squirmed on her seat and crossed herself.

Sister Ria walked on.

There were hat-makers, offering everything from handsome wide-brimmed Mexican sombreros to European fedoras and berets, and there were tailors, butchers, silversmiths, leather-makers, confectioners and potters. The gaudy colours, the sounds of shoppers and livestock mixing with the voices of the proprietors hawking their wares brought back memories. Good memories of her and her sister Milagros dragging their poor governess, Leonora, up and down this dirt street in search of some grand prize of their imagination. And memories of her father bringing her here mornings so that he could sit in the cafés and read the newspapers brought off the ships anchored in San Pedro harbour – the same mornings Milagros was taken by the nursemaids to Mercer's school to take dance lessons.

She had hated those mornings among the old men of

the pueblo. Her father had always made her remove her hat at the tables. And no matter how many years she had come here, no matter how many times they had seen her, the men always gawked at her shaved head.

Sister Ria concentrated her thoughts on Milagros' dancing. Her older sister had been wonderful at it, had shown her the steps for the waltz, the bolero and the jota, the two of them practising at night. Sister Ria swallowed hard. She had never danced with a man. She wondered what it would have been like. Something about that silly fact saddened her and she closed her eyes and shook her head. None of it mattered now, she belonged to Christ.

She turned in a slow circle, trying to forget the past, focusing on the world around her. Slowly, the look and smells and sounds of the market seeped into her, making her feel as though at least some good pieces of this life she had known as a girl survived, and would exist no matter what happened to her or her father. She began moving again, passing by the fruiterers' stalls, carefully examining the size and quality of the oranges and lemons, peaches and apricots. It had been a good year for orchard crops. From the large size of the apricots and peaches, she estimated that there had been over 18 inches of rain – when the average was somewhere close to 13 in a normal growing season. Yes, a good year.

Then suddenly she stopped and studied a cluster of grapes, her body tensing, sensing she was being watched. But when she looked up, no one beyond the shopkeepers seemed to be paying her any mind. Then she saw a small man in a brown suit and black fedora standing and looking at her near the tinsmith's stall. But he turned away and she was not certain.

She moved on down the road and sat on an old wooden

bench under the shade of a mulberry tree, gazing at the sights of the marketplace and wondering if the canasta and checkers players still came here in the afternoons to test their skills. Not far down the road in an empty lot were a number of Mexican men and women sitting in a row like school children in stiff-backed chairs, listening to a young man with glasses in a clean white shirt reading the newspaper out loud. She smiled in recognition – things hadn't changed that much. There was still a Spanish feel to the pueblo, in spite of the Americanos.

The market was filling up with people. The Mexican men were for the most part labourers dressed in rough cotton clothes, the women wearing bright dresses, shawls and straw hats. There were also Chinese women in colourful tight knee-length silk dresses that were split daringly up the side, with beautiful paper parasols open on their shoulders as protection from the sun. Then there were the Americans and Europeans, fairly large numbers of them for the hour, the women wearing high-collared dresses and hats with long silk ribbon ties and white gloves. She stretched the tenseness from her shoulders. Where was Milagros? She had always been so close to him. Why had she not come?

It made no sense.

The brothel where Dorothy Regal had been murdered stood in bright morning sunlight at the end of a small bricked alleyway known as Strand's Road. Sister Ria was standing at the bottom of a flight of wooden stairs that ran up the side of the building, hesitating and uncertain why. She had witnessed hundreds of death chambers. Still, she hesitated.

There was no one around. And no sounds came from inside the building. The sign on the rope at the bottom of the stairs finally stiffened her resolve and started her moving.

Keep Out
By Order of the Department of Police
City of Los Angeles

Something about the sign seemed as cold and uncaring as Chief Hood, and she quickly ducked under the rope, raising the hem of her robe and trotting defiantly up the stairs. Fernando too bounded quickly up the wooden steps behind her. She tried the door.

Open.

She stepped inside and the old cat shot through the opening before she shut the door. The room was dark and Sister Ria pulled some wallpaper off the window glass and stood letting her eyes adjust to the morning shadows. The room was small and cheap and filled with the heavy smell of human sweat and perfume. She glanced at the neatly made bed and tried to keep from thinking what had gone on here. Then she looked down at the floor and jumped.

They had not cleaned up the blood and she could see the outline of Dorothy Regal's head and shoulders clearly in the brown stain. She brought a hand to her throat. The girl was even smaller than she appeared in Hood's photograph, the span of her shoulders childlike. 'You poor thing,' Sister Ria whispered. She crossed herself and knelt down beside the blood stain and clasped her hands. Though she had witnessed death in a myriad of forms, she knew she would never get used to it – that each time it would tear away a piece of her heart. Fernando sniffed at the edges of the stain.

As she was praying, Sister Ria reached down for her

61

wooden crucifix that hung on the cincture around her waist. Her hand groped for it for a moment before she realized it was not there. She pulled the cord up in front of her face. It had been cut, the crucifix gone. He must have done it while she was asleep in the hallway. 'Damn you,' she muttered and then said, 'Forgive me, Lord,' and returned to her prayer for Dorothy.

Sister Ria had been in the room for a long time, just looking at the small cramped compartment with its iron bed, table and chair, brass kerosene lamp. She did not know what to do next. She had searched every inch of it and then hunted through a stack of Dorothy's papers in a box on the table, mostly playbills from local theatres. She had found only one thing that seemed worth keeping: a small slip of paper that had been torn from a writing tablet.

She unfolded it and read the printed words: *Brown cutaway* – written in a blue ink. Then lower down the small slip was pencilled the word: *Curandera* – that meant a female healer. Had the dead woman been sick? The only healer Sister Ria could remember was an ancient hag by the name of Nachita, rumoured to have been the oldest woman in the world. Sister Ria had no idea what the words might mean. But she held on to the paper. The police appeared to have removed everything else from this small dirty room filled with sadness and lost dreams. Still, she lingered. Did she want to pray once more? Perhaps that was it.

She saw it as she was kneeling.

It was barely visible under the edge of the pillow, the corner of a book. Sister Ria picked it up: *The Poems of Alfred, Lord Tennyson – Volume II.* She rubbed her fingertips over the soft leather binding and stared at the gold letters, a small pocket edition of love poems in a beautiful leather cover. Something about it did not make sense. It was expensive. It did not fit in this cheap room. If Dorothy Regal had loved Tennyson, there were canvas- or paper-covered editions.

Sister Ria shook her head. That wasn't fair, she told herself. Perhaps this was Dorothy Regal's only way to touch something fine and good in her sad life. She thumbed through the book. There was no inscription, no initials of ownership, nothing. She placed the piece of paper inside the little book and slipped them both into the pocket of her robe and began to carefully move through the apartment again. This time, she knew what she was looking for: *Volume I.*

It was not there.

Lord – please help me.

Sister Ria stood waiting for some sign, some inclination in her heart. When none came, when the frustration of having been drawn into this futile search for answers she was certain would lead nowhere soared inside her head, she snapped, 'I can't help him.'

SIX

Sister Ria was searching the house for her father. He had left discarded sketches in the central courtyard, tossed away near the two iron lions that guarded the path to the stables, and strewn over the floor of the loggia.

She found him in the small sitting room next to the library, stretched out on a meridienne sketching furiously on a stack of papers. His large wooden painting easel had been set up nearby. She pulled a chair close and sat facing him. He was dressed as a Catholic priest in a bone-white surplice with a purple sash tied around his waist, a large silver crucifix dangling from a heavy chain around his neck. Strange as it seemed, he was wearing a Jewish yarmulke on his head. Though she had intentionally scraped the chair over the tiled floor, he did not look up at her.

She studied his face. He had aged. The skin around his mouth and eyes was sagging and deeply wrinkled and he had a sickly sallow cast to him. His eyebrows were flecked with silver, his hair thin to the point where she could see scalp. But there was something about him – the essence of him – that had not changed. She saw it in the expression in his eyes, a mixture of energy and fire.

'Father –'

He did not look up.

When he worked at his sketching and painting, no one dared to disturb him. Aba knew to keep the servants quietly occupied in other parts of the hacienda and to turn visitors away. When he had finished working he would retire to his room or the gardens. Sister Ria cleared her throat loudly. She didn't care what he demanded. As if in response, he crumpled a sheet of paper and tossed it to the floor and went back to sketching.

'Did you kill that girl?' she asked.

He looked up at her, eyebrows slightly raised.

'What girl?'

She stood over him shaking her head. 'Father, please do not play games. Please. The girl they are going to execute you for killing. Did you kill her?'

'I thought you had come for an apology for your poor little hurts. I liked you so much better then. You've become tiresome.'

'I don't care what I've become. I want to know if you killed Dorothy Regal.'

'Why are you dressed like that?' he asked. 'There is much that needs doing.' He tipped his head back and scanned the ceiling of the room for a moment, as if searching for the small lizards that sometimes scaled the walls, then he seemed to remember that she was standing in front of him and he looked at her. 'I will trade you your robe for a seventeenth-century satin cloak with jabot and wide sleeves.' He examined her vestments with an appraising eye, then continued, 'But only if you include your headpiece – what is it called?'

'It's called a wimple.'

'Will you include it?'

'I do not want one of your silly outfits.'

'Then may I borrow yours?'

'No. You may not. But I do want you to return my crucifix – the wooden crucifix you stole,' she said, holding up the end of her cincture. 'And I want you to answer me about the woman.'

'It is a very nice satin cloak.'

'I don't care,' she mumbled. Then slowly, the memory flooded over her.

It was a lovely spring day, the fields aflame with flowing seas of golden poppies, the sky cloudless, the air warm but not hot. The children were playing a tag game with green ribbons in the gravelled front yard of the Banning hacienda. They were there in celebration of Isadora's friend Celeste Banning's twelfth birthday. All were dressed in their finest, the girls in sun dresses and bonnets with long, lovely ribbons and white gloves, and the boys, including Isadora, wearing sombreros, short jackets and fine pants. She had worn the clothing of boys for so long now that it attracted little attention. Isadora was 'it' – and she stood in the centre of the sunlit square with her eyes closed counting out loud as the rules required.

When she opened her eyes, she was surprised to see the governesses herding the other children quickly into the hacienda, staring back over their shoulders at something behind Isadora. She turned and looked. It was the first time she had ever seen him masquerade outside of La Cienega, and she wanted to run and never stop running.

The Patrón was sitting on a beautiful Arabian stallion, wearing a black satin woman's riding habit, with a feathered top hat and veil, white waistcoat and red cravat, his skirt-covered bare leg draped over the pommel hook of a woman's side-saddle. 'Do you like my outfit?' he asked, smiling down at her.

The whispers and giggling began again . . .

Sister Ria focused her eyes hard on her father. He had gone back to his sketching.

'Much has been neglected by you,' he said, smearing charcoal expertly over the paper with the palm of his hand.

She shook her head, 'No. This isn't about me. I need to know. Did you kill that girl?'

'Have you come to disturb my work?'

'No. I came because of Mother. Now, tell me, are you a murderer?'

Don Maximiato was staring at the ceiling again. Then he looked at her. 'You were never one to stick with a task.'

'How dare you!'

'This is a sanctuary. Please keep your voice down.'

'This is not a sanctuary. You are not a priest. You are simply mad.'

'I am.'

'You are what? Mad?'

'A holy man.'

'You forget that I am your daughter. I grew up in this house. I know you.'

He stared at her.

'You take lovers,' she said. 'What kind of holy man takes lovers?'

'Not lovers, whores.'

'Whatever. You are not a holy man.'

He appeared to drift into sleep.

Fear and frustration building inside her, Sister Ria turned and went to his easel and took a brush, dabbing it into a jar of black paint. Then she walked to a nearby wall and brushed a large number 7 on the stark white plaster. She turned around and faced him. Her hands were trembling.

'Perhaps that will help you – you have seven days left of life. Do you understand? Seven days!'

He had opened his eyes and was looking down at his papers again.

'Why does the Almighty hide?' he asked. 'Is he ashamed of his creation?'

'Please, just answer me. Did you kill Dorothy Regal?'

He was suddenly as excited as a child. 'Soon God will take me in his embrace.'

She stood up slowly, bracing herself on the arm of the chair, moving as with great difficulty.

'Yes, Father, very soon,' she said softly. 'I pray so.'

She started to leave the room, then noticed that she had got paint on her hand. She went back and picked up the paper he had tossed on the floor and opened it up. She froze. It was the same face she had seen in the police photograph – Dorothy Regal. He had sketched Dorothy Regal's head and shoulders – the dead girl smiling. Sister Ria balled the paper in her hand, squeezing it until her knuckles were white, and threw it at him, the paper bouncing off his head. He didn't flinch. She was sobbing without sound. Then she heard two sharp raps on the heavy tile floor and Sister Ria turned and saw Aba standing in the doorway.

SEVEN

The afternoon light was creating a sepia tone on the towering walls of the hacienda's library, making the lovely room with its long reading table and lacquered globes look like an old tintype. Fernando was batting a small white feather up and down the length of the table. Sister Ria took a deep breath and gazed at the floor-to-ceiling bookshelves surrounding her. Like her father's life, there was no order to them – more than a hundred years of Lugo family records and reading material. She shook her head. It didn't matter. She had to concentrate – had to know if the companion volume of Tennyson was here.

She climbed to the top of the oak library ladder and began to run her fingertips over the titles. Finished with the first row, she moved down a step and did the same to the second. Earlier, while he was in the garden painting, she had quickly searched his cluttered bedroom and found nothing. Then she had done the same to the other rooms of the hacienda. Again, nothing.

She was inching her way down the rows of books when her eyes locked on a thin volume. She pulled it out. Unlike the others, it had been recently dusted. Her heart was starting to race: *The Anatomy of Human Dissection.*

'Is there a specific book you are searching for?' Aba asked.

Sister Ria jumped and turned on the ladder as if she had been caught stealing. 'Pardon?' she said, sliding the book back into its place on the shelf.

'A book,' Aba said, shooing Fernando off the table and leaning on her cane. 'Is there a specific one that I can find for you?'

'No,' she said, trying to collect herself. 'I'm just looking them over. Is that a problem, Aba?'

The old woman stiffened at the remark. 'None whatsoever, Isadora. This is your home. You may do as you wish. The problem lies in your behaviour towards your father.'

Sister Ria began to search the titles again. 'I apologize.'

'You don't mean that, child. So don't say it to me.'

Sister Ria was still facing the wall of books, when she said, 'He sketched the face of the dead woman, Dorothy Regal.'

'He sketches many things. He is interested in many things.'

'In dead women?'

'I do not care for your insinuation, Isadora.'

Sister Ria was suddenly angry and she pulled the book from the shelf and held it down to the woman.

'Your insolence is not becoming the daughter of the Patrón,' Aba said, glancing at the book. 'He has always been a student of the human body. He is an artist.'

'Where was he the night of her death?'

'I'm sure he was in his room.'

'Did you see him there?'

'You know that I do not enter the Patrón's quarters when he has retired for the night.'

'So you don't know?'

'I know the Patrón.' Aba cocked her head and squinted at Sister Ria. 'Do you not, child?'

'No,' Sister Ria said.

EIGHT

The restaurant was French and built around a handsome courtyard of fine trees and thick beds of yellow lilies, night-blooming jasmine, white phlox and spires of deep pink foxglove. It was late evening and the coloured lanterns strung through the branches of the trees cast a beautiful romantic glow over the grounds. The dining room with its perfectly clean white tablecloths and wavering candle-light opened onto this square, the air smelling of jasmine mixed with the ever-present odour of sage from the hills. The restaurant was on the ground floor of the Pico Hotel across the street from the town plaza.

Sister Ria was waiting for the young newspaper editor, Clemente Rojo, whom she had spoken to that morning in the offices of the Mexican newspaper, *La Verdad,* to join her for dinner, replaying the afternoon over and over in her mind. She had learned nothing. Volume I was not in the hacienda – all she had found was the book on surgical procedures.

The muscles of her back tightened. The little book on dissection had been recently handled, and both of Dorothy

72

Regal's carotid arteries had been severed by a deep arcing cut, the woman neatly gutted, her child sliced from her womb. Not hacked, sliced. Sister Ria bit down on her lip and clenched her hands as if she was going to hit something.

Aba is right.

Having a book on dissection did not make him a murderer. He was an artist, and artists studied the human body. Leonardo da Vinci had paid grave-robbers to bring him fresh corpses to examine.

Not certain whether she should be comforted by this last thought, Sister Ria smoothed a pure white napkin over her lap, running her fingertips over the soft material. In another room someone was playing most beautifully the Largo from *Winter* by Vivaldi on a harp, the lilting notes drifting softly on the air. Sister Ria's table was on the veranda and she was drinking chilled water and watching the full moon rising over the distant San Gabriel Mountains and thinking about the girl's face in her father's drawing, wondering if he could possibly be mad enough to murder. Aba had told her that Dorothy Regal's death-photograph had been run in the newspapers for weeks during the trial and that she was certain that was where the Patrón had seen it. She shivered and forced her thoughts on.

The evening air felt brisk and clean. She might be sitting in a restaurant in any fine hotel in Europe. It was amazing, this transformation of the pueblo. She took a sip of her water. Then guilt struck her.

Her fellow Sisters would have sat this night at the long convent table in the grey stone refectory drinking cheap wine with their meagre meal because neither the village nor the city's water was fit to drink. What was she doing, dressed in this lovely new habit of fine light linen cloth that Aba had had sewn for her – drinking pure water with crystals of ice floating in it, awaiting a meal whose cost would provide a year of food for a family in Poona? She had vowed to live as the poor lived, not in the luxury of her former life. Was she ready to renounce her sacred vows? She stiffened at the thought.

'Are you OK?' Clemente Rojo, the newspaper editor, asked, standing at the edge of the table.

'Yes, I'm fine,' she said, releasing her grip on the table-cloth, 'just tired.'

'Tired, perhaps – but you look lovely, Sister,' he said, bowing slightly.

She reddened, wondering if she would ever get used to being openly stared at or commented on by men. 'It is good to see you again, Mr Rojo.'

'Clemente, please,' he said. 'Where is Happy?'

'Pardon?'

'Happy Fernando. I expected to see him curled around the salt shaker.'

She laughed. The old cat had taken a nap in the centre of the young editor's desk that morning, just as he had on Chief Hood's. She guessed he liked desks, or perhaps he just liked to annoy people. It was probably the latter.

'He asked me to send his regrets – he did not have proper attire.'

Clemente smiled. 'Our loss.'

Clemente Rojo didn't look to be any older than she was, though he carried himself like an old man with an almost humorous seriousness that spoke of grave concerns and heavy responsibilities. Small and thin, he wore heavy steel-framed glasses that he periodically pushed up his nose as though they had been borrowed from someone else.

And while he rarely smiled, there was something warm and sincere about him. She liked him.

Unlike the other men in the restaurant, most of whom were Americans or Europeans, Clemente was dressed in a beautifully embroidered Mexican short-waisted jacket in black velvet and tight-fitting pantaloons that flared over a pair of handsome black dress boots. Clothing she also had once worn. Ignoring this last thought, she reached across the table and handed him the stack of newspaper editorials on the trial of her father that he had given her that morning. 'Thank you for these.'

'Useful?'

'Very.' She paused. 'But unfortunately I don't have any real answers about what happened that night.'

'Your meeting with Chief Hood?'

'The police believe everything they found points to my father.'

Clemente watched her for a moment. 'And you don't?'

'Nothing I saw or heard proves my father's guilt.' She took a sip of water. 'I am not saying he's innocent, I'm just saying they didn't have enough to convict him. Aside from some of his possessions, they have nothing – no convincing explanation for why he would have done it, no witness who saw him with the woman the night she was murdered. They don't even know whether or not he knew her. And more to the point, their investigation appears to have been very superficial.'

Clemente picked up a piece of paper listing the restaurant's wines, waiting for her to continue.

She hesitated for a moment but could see no reason not to tell the man. 'I went to her room today. I found a book there under her pillow. The police hadn't even stripped her bed.' She paused. 'If they hadn't even bothered to look in her bed – in a room that tiny – how thorough could their search have been?'

Clemente didn't comment on the police work, he just looked over the edge of the wine list at her. 'A book. Why would that be important?'

'I don't believe it belonged to her. It was a book of Tennyson poems, expensive, leather bound, one of two volumes.'

'And you think it belonged to the killer?'

'I don't know. All I know is that the police should have found it – and at least questioned who it belonged to.'

Rojo pursed his lips and sat thinking, 'Volume I or Volume II?'

She evaded the question, staring down at her hands on the table. She wasn't certain why. When she looked back up the editor was carefully scanning the wine list, as if searching for the key to life. 'You're smart not to believe all that Hood tells you,' he said finally, his eyes still fixed on the list of wines.

She tensed. 'Why is that, sir?'

'His department is corrupt.'

Sister Ria felt the muscles across the top of her shoulders tighten even more and she continued to stare at the man. 'Are you saying he framed my father?'

'No. Just that he is capable of it.'

They spent the next few minutes talking about the poor condition of law enforcement in the City of Los Angeles, Hood and his department, injustices committed against the Mexicans and Chinese in town. The more Clemente talked, the more Sister Ria liked the young editor, finding his conversation candidly fresh and interesting. But it was not helping her.

'You are not saying that he framed my father?'

'No. I know nothing like that. Just that Hood doesn't care much for Mexicans or Chinese, which would help explain why the police didn't do a thorough job investigating Dorothy Regal's murder once they found your father's clothes and the knife.'

Clemente went back to studying the wines again. Finally he placed the page on the table and instead of smiling as most people would, he frowned at her and said, 'He is a very odd man, your father.'

Sister Ria pressed her lips together and forced herself to smile.

Clemente straightened his napkin and looked grave again. 'One day he arrived in court dressed like a pirate with a tri-cornered hat and an eye patch and knee-pants, stockings and brass-buckled shoes.' The man waited a moment, 'Another day he came dressed like a woman you'd expect to see at the Moulin Rouge.'

Sister Ria looked as if none of this came as a surprise. 'Did he always –'

'Dress so exotically,' she offered.

'Yes, that's a good way to put it,' he agreed.

'Always,' she said, shaking her head at the lunacy of a man on trial for his life behaving this way. But then neither the trial nor the people conducting it meant anything to him. No one, she knew, meant anything to him.

She least of all.

Sister Ria had left the serious young newspaper man inside the restaurant interviewing a Chicago businessman who had just arrived in town. She had learned interesting details from Clemente over dinner but nothing new, nothing other than speculation about the death of Dorothy Regal.

It was after ten and she was standing in the crowded

77

lobby of the Pico Hotel thinking through her conversation with Clemente Rojo and wanting to be away from the noise and alone with her thoughts. She walked out the hotel's front door and crossed the street to the old plaza gardens. The night sky was sprayed with flecks of gold across a vast black wash and she knelt on the grass and tipped her head up at the stars, and prayed for an answer. Any answer – just something that would put an end to the torrent of questions raging through her mind.

Nothing came to her. She struggled to her feet and moved into the darkness, making her way down a brick pathway, her habit snagging on the branches growing over the walk, moving trance-like through the maze of footpaths that ran through stands of overgrown bushes and trees, wandering aimlessly.

She pushed open a wooden gate and moved past a flush of pink oleanders and towering, sharp-bladed agave plants. Peach trees, heavy with fruit, lined the other side of the walkway, the straight lines of the path softened by the masses of flowers that spilled over the bricks. She continued walking without any sense of direction – just walking, as if unable to stop.

The night air was cool and she pulled her shawl tighter around her shoulders. Then she suddenly stopped moving and stood in the darkness. When she finally started walking again, she was listening closely to the night, staring at the bricks beneath her feet. Someone was moving in the darkness with her, matching their steps to hers. She was certain of it.

She turned around. The path behind her was empty. But she sensed something in the darkness and turned back and started quickly away, trying to determine where she should head.

She had moved only a short distance when she heard the sound again: quick, careful footsteps following her. She stopped. The sound stopped. That was all it took. Yanking her veil quickly over her face to mask the white cloth of her headband, she hurriedly wormed her way deep into the bushes beside the path.

She held her breath and waited.

Nothing. Knowing any movement would be seen, she froze and squinted through the gauze-like screen of cloth, vegetation and shadows. There was no one on the path. Ten minutes. Still nothing. She was tired and jumpy. Perhaps she had only imagined the sound. She continued to wait. Nothing seemed out of place in the gardens or the night. Then, as she was getting ready to leave her hiding place, something suddenly stirred the bushes behind her and a hand slid over her mouth.

In the midst of her rising fright came the whispered words, 'Do you know me, nun?'

Sister Ria clamped down on the air in her throat and held it and shook her head no.

'Have you not sinned?'

Sister Ria froze. 'Yes,' she stammered.

'I thought so,' the voice whispered in her ear.

Panic surging in her like waves against a sea wall, she instinctively stamped the heavy heel of her convent shoe down hard on the foot of the person behind her, and jammed her buttocks backwards with a hard thrusting motion. It was a trick she had been taught as a child by one of La Cienega's Basque sheep-herders, who had rescued her from a beating at the hands of some street boys who had bullied her into a fight. When she heard the wooshing of exhaled air and felt the arm losing its grip on her, she whirled to throw a punch.

She froze – fighting off a yell of surprise.
'Milagros?'
Her sister was hopping around, holding her foot and laughing.

NINE

'I can't believe it's you,' Sister Ria said, pressing the fingers of both hands against her lips. She gazed at her sister's face in the soft yellow lamplight of the hotel room. 'How did you find me?'

Milagros was sitting in a chair, massaging her foot. 'I saw a nun praying like the holy Madonna across the street from the hotel and figured it could only be my little sister,' she said, examining her toes. 'When you headed into the plaza I thought I'd have some fun with you. I had no idea you would break my foot.' She forced a laugh. 'You nuns are supposed to be gentle creatures.'

Neither of them was ready to talk about it.

'I hope I broke it,' Sister Ria said.

Milagros stretched her toes slowly.

'You're not as quick as you once were,' Sister Ria teased.

'Old age, Izzie,' Milagros sighed dramatically.

Sister Ria loved her sister deeply. Loyal Milagros. She had always been there for her, had stood shoulder to shoulder with her whenever the pueblo's street boys teased and bullied her, throwing rocks and taunting her and challenging her to fist fights. She and Milagros had lost most of the battles, but they never ran, a fact which drove their young governess, Leonora, frantic. Milagros had also taken her part with their father, bravely standing up, even as a child, to the man's wrath.

She leaned forward and kissed the top of Milagros' head. 'You were always my heroine. What was that game we played?' she asked, still avoiding the subject on both their minds.

Milagros smiled sadly. '*Las Animas Perdidas* – The Lost Souls.'

'Yes,' Sister Ria said. Milagros had changed into a night-gown and satin robe, her hair in a soft pompadour that showed her magnificent face with its delicate bone structure, wide eyes, full lips. 'You were *La Conquistadora* – Our Lady of Victory,' Sister Ria continued, 'and I was your trusted helper *Santa Osita* – Saint Little Bear. You wore that wonderful blue cape we stole from Father.'

She watched Milagros brush away a gleaming black strand of hair, her features careworn.

As usual, Millie put up a good front, smiling through her sadness. 'And you wore that smelly sheepskin that Aba had dyed black. With those skinny legs of yours you looked like a woolly aardvark.'

'Thank you,' Sister Ria laughed and bowed solemnly. '*Oye! Oye!* – Hear! Hear! The great La Conquistadora has come to fight the pagan *Moros y Turcos* – Moors and Turks – to save *El Nino Perdido* – The Lost Boy.'

Milagros chuckled.

Sister Ria continued in a soft voice, 'I present the Grand Conquistadora, *rueque para su alma* – pray for her soul.' Sister Ria tipped her head back and squinted at the ceiling. 'What was our flower?'

'*La Rosa de Castilla* – the Rose of Castile.'

'Yes. Whenever you saved someone I would present you with La Rosa de Castilla.' Sister Ria looked at Milagros. 'You deserve a dead petunia tonight.'

'I'd rather have a cast for my foot.'

They held each other and cried, the years dropping away.

'Milagros, thank God you are here,' Sister Ria whispered. Her older sister had always been so capable. Sister Ria's chest tightened. Only once had she ever known Millie to panic.

It was the middle of a hot summer afternoon. They had slipped away from their nursemaids who were taking their midday rest on the veranda. Having successfully escaped, they gathered their costumes and ran to play at the large brick cistern behind the horse barn. It was a perfect place for their favourite version of La Conquistadora: La Pirata – The Pirate. They had brought Emilia, the five-year-old daughter of the servant Rosa, to play the part of El Niño Perdido. And now Emilia was standing out on the centre of the boardwalk that spanned the dark waters, a rope tied around her waist, the other end held by Milagros, the little girl looking dutifully frightened and ready to be saved by the great Conquistadora. Emilia had played the role many times and loved it every bit as much as the sisters did. Then the frown left the little girl's face and she was laughing and slapping her hands together.

'*Silencio,*' *Isadora said.* '*You must look scared.*'

'*Yes,*' *Milagros added,* '*you are about to walk the ship's plank to a watery death.*'

Emilia looked appropriately solemn again and took a step forward.

'*Wait,*' *Isadora said, stopping the game and crawling*

*down the cistern's ladder and running to cut a rose from
the garden that she could present to La Conquistadora
when she had saved the child. For Isadora, it was always
the best part of the game, this solemn ceremony that
honoured the sister she loved so dearly.*

*Even now, thinking back to that day, she could still feel
the horrible emptiness inside her when she climbed back
up onto the brick wall of the cistern. Emilia was no longer
on the plank, the safety rope gone as well, Milagros just
standing and staring down at the dark waters.*

Milagros was leaning back in a large wing chair nervously inhaling from a cigarette in a silver holder, her
features changing until they took on a fixed look of blunt
panic. Sister Ria knelt and grasped her hand.

They were both still trying to avoid it.

A smile softened Milagros' features and she pulled her
hand free and slowly stroked her sister's cheek. 'I still can't
believe you are a nun – little Santa Osita who stole many
hundreds of galletas dulces from the poor bakers. Surely
you will go to Hell for that.' Then the smile left her face,
replaced by a deep sadness.

Sister Ria stood and kissed the top of her sister's
head again. Her gaze wandered to an open closet and
a rack of expensive clothes and close by a pile of beautiful silk undergarments – the fine trappings of the wife
of a San Francisco banker. 'You've been here a while,'
she said.

It was time.

'Yes. I've been hounding judges, politicians, police –
anybody who might know something about that night.'
She wrapped her arms around her middle as if her stomach
hurt.

'You haven't seen Father?'

84

'I've had to be strong. Seeing him would break my heart.'

Sister Ria watched Milagros for a time before she said, 'I went to her room today.'

'Whose room?'

'Dorothy Regal's. Have you seen it?'

Milagros shook her head.

'It's just a single room above a brothel. The poor child. She had nothing.'

'He didn't kill her.'

'I found a book –' She paused. 'A leather-bound book, Volume II of Tennyson's love poems. I don't think it was hers. It might belong to her killer.'

Milagros was gazing at the floor.

'I searched the library at La Cienega for Volume I. It wasn't there.'

'Because he didn't kill her.' She looked exhausted.

Sister Ria continued talking, as if she had to get these things out. 'There was a slip of paper on her table with writing on it that said, *Brown cutaway*. And on the bottom, *Curandera*. Does that make any sense to you?'

Milagros shook her head. 'The curandera could be Nachita, that old beggar woman who pretended to be a healer and diviner. The one the mission priests condemned as a witch.'

Sister Ria nodded. 'I thought of her. She can't still be alive, can she?'

Milagros shrugged, then she looked up at her sister. 'Father didn't kill that woman.'

'I wish I could be so certain.'

Compassion altered Milagros' features. 'You can't keep condemning him.'

'It's more than that,' Sister Ria said, kneeling before her

sister again, placing her hands on both sides of Milagros'
head. 'Milagros, listen to me.'

Their eyes met.

'He's not right,' she said. 'Worse than when we were
children.'

'He didn't do it.'

'Millie, he's not right.'

'He didn't do it,' Milagros snapped.

'How can you be so sure?'

Milagros hesitated. 'Because I know who did.'

'Millie?'

'Father didn't kill her. Someone else did.'

Sister Ria studied her sister's face for a long time. 'Who?'

'No, Izzie.'

'What do you mean, no? Tell me who.'

'I don't want you involved.'

'Tell me.'

'Two men.'

'What men?'

Milagros rubbed her forehead, her eyes moving slowly
over her sister's face. 'They planned it a year ago.' She
was wringing her hands now.

'Why?'

'To get rid of Father.'

'Why would they want to get rid of Father?'

'Two years ago they won the city's street light contract.'
Milagros was gazing at the floor again.

'So?'

'They had been buying local tar to burn as fuel, but it
caused a noxious cloud to spread over the town and the city
banned its use. Now they have to ship coal in from Australia,
and they're going broke.' She picked up the cigarette in the
holder and puffed anxiously until the ash turned orange.

Confusion deepened on Sister Ria's face. 'What does that have to do with Father?'

'I'll tell you, but only if you promise to leave.'

'Millie!'

'At least promise you'll think about leaving.'

'I'll think about it. Now tell me.'

'Geologists say there is coal under the water at La Brea Hoya.'

Sister Ria frowned. La Brea Hoya – *the tar pit* – was a swamp marsh on the eastern edge of La Cienega. The oily waters were considered useless except for the gummy tar that bubbled to its surface and was used to caulk barrels and roofs.

Milagros took a nervous draw on her cigarette. 'They offered Father $50,000 for five acres and the right to mine it. Then $75,000. But you know Papa.'

'Why didn't you tell the police?'

'I did.'

'And?'

'They laughed.'

'Why?'

'These are prominent men – Americans.'

Sister Ria thought of her conversation with Clemente Rojo and the muscle beneath her eye began to twitch. 'He drew Dorothy Regal's picture this afternoon,' she said weakly.

Milagros' voice rose in frustration. 'Father didn't kill her, Izzie.' She stopped and collected herself. 'They sent a man to me last week. I told him I knew what they had done, that I wouldn't sell either.' She looked up at her sister. 'They'll try to kill me now.'

'Milagros, stop it!'

'And now you're here, Izzie.' The words seemed to float in the room.

For an instant Sister Ria thought of the bloody cross that had been made on the wall of her bedroom and of the odd sensation of being watched that she had felt in the marketplace. But she quickly shoved these thoughts aside, certain in her heart that her father had killed the rooster in her room. The other she put down to her own imagination.

'Milagros, that's silly.'

Milagros shut her eyes and held up her hands to stop her sister from saying anything more. 'They are desperate. You have to understand that. You have to be frightened of it.'

Sister Ria began to pace. When she finally stopped she was standing by a small desk beneath the front window. She rubbed the edge of a silver frame containing a photograph of Milagros and her San Francisco banker husband, Robert Sullivan. Milagros had met him twelve years before at a dinner party while she was attending Mrs Andre's Finishing School in San Francisco – and married him one month later. Sister Ria had never seen his picture before. Milagros had never brought him home. She didn't blame her – their home life was not easily explained. She jumped when Milagros touched her shoulder.

Milagros hugged her from behind and then let her go and lit another cigarette. 'Go back to Spain. Or India. Anywhere. Just go.'

'We always stood together.'

'We always will. But not here, Izzie. I'm leaving tomorrow – to see the Governor in Sacramento to try to get a stay of execution. It's not safe here any longer.' She wiped her face with her hand, her eyes narrowing as she fought the tears. 'Then I'll go home to San Francisco. I've asked my husband to hire new detectives. I'm afraid the ones here have been bought off.' She looked at her sister. 'Please, Izzie.'

Sister Ria pulled herself up to her full height and turned to face her sister. 'Millie, give me their names.'

'Just leave.'

'Their names, Millie.'

The convent at Poona seemed so distant, she wondered if she could ever return. She had just reached the street in front of the Pico Hotel and was looking up at Milagros' room. The window was dark. There was something terribly final in that black pane of glass.

She stood for a long time in front of the hotel, her thoughts lingering over this too-brief reunion with Milagros. They had hugged in the hallway outside her room, crying and laughing, and then Milagros had pulled quickly away and said, 'Go, Izzie, before you're hurt.'

Sister Ria had gazed into her sister's lovely face and whispered, 'I present to you La Conquistadora. She fears nothing. *Rueque para su alma.* Pray for her soul.'

The wind was blowing in from the high deserts to the north, blasting bits of dirt and dust over the roadway. Sister Ria was still standing in the street, reluctant to leave, looking up at Milagros' room, praying for her. Then she unfolded the piece of paper Milagros had given her and read the two names: L. Summerville and Samuel Atkins. They meant nothing to her.

The wind rose as Sister Ria crawled onto the buggy seat and started the little grey horse towards home. She watched the shadows along the empty street, remembering what Millie had said about the danger, the clop of the horse comforting.

She stopped the carriage at the corner of Santa Cruz and Mesa and looked back at the hotel. Milagros' room was still dark. 'La Conquistadora,' she whispered. 'Rueque para su alma.'

The buildings and sidewalks of the American part of town were empty of people and lit by lamplight. She glanced at the closest glass globe, watching its flame hissing in the night, the yellow glow ominous now. Down the street she could see the dark roof line of the headquarters building of the Los Angeles Gas Company.

Could Milagros be right?

No, she whispered. Milagros just loved their father too much to be able to believe him guilty of murder, that was all.

Sister Ria was about to slap the reins on the rump of the little carriage horse when she heard the sound. She sat up straighter. The wind was rising and falling as it shot through the gaps between the buildings and she wasn't certain what she had heard. Then it came again – shrill piping above the gusts. 'Holy Sister.' The voice of a child.

'Yes?'

Nothing.

'Hello?' she called.

Sister Ria reined the horse in a wide arc back towards the mouth of the alley where she thought she had heard the voice, guiding the animal into the narrow passageway as far as the faint slice of lamplight, then halting. The walls of the buildings broke the force of the gale but they also trapped the floating dirt, creating a thick fog of drifting silt in the dark passage.

'Child, are you in there?'

Sister Ria squinted into the haze, searching for movement, a reflection of light, anything that might be a lost or injured child. There was nothing.

She could hear water dripping.

'Say something.'

Silence.

She waited until she was convinced she had been imagining things and began to back the little horse out of the alleyway.

'Holy Sister!'

The small voice had leaped out of the wind and darkness at her and she jumped down from the carriage and moved towards the sound, her eyes sensing objects in the murky gloom.

'Where are you? Talk to me!'

She was deep into the alley, choking on dust and standing in a muddy pool of inch-deep water, peering into the darkness, her mind confused. The voice had sounded so close and so desperate. Had she walked past the child in the murky darkness? She began to retrace her steps, slowly searching foot by foot for an open pit or doorway, any place where a child might be hiding or trapped. Nothing. Then she remembered Millie's warning and she straightened up, sweat breaking over her skin.

If she wanted to get killed, this was a good place. The buildings were windowless sheets of brick, the alley as lonely and dangerous as any she had seen in Poona or Calcutta. The walls and wind would smother any sounds of struggle. No one would hear.

She did not want to get killed.

She would find a policeman to search the alley with her. Slowly, she backed towards the carriage. The stench of raw sewage burned her eyes. 'Child,' she called one more time, 'can you hear me?' She stopped and listened and thought she heard voices in the darkness. But it was only the wind on brick. Was that all she had heard in the first place? She was no longer certain, and fear was growing inside her. She began walking hurriedly towards the carriage.

When she heard them again, the words were filled with panic, 'Help me – Holy Sister!'

She had turned back and was running now, feeling down the brick wall with her hands, jumping over pools of water and piles of garbage, her body drenched in sweat, mumbling: 'Lord, Lord, Lord –' She had almost reached the end of the alley when she saw a broken place in the wall a few yards ahead, a dark entry – but not completely dark: a vague glow emanated from the tunnel-like passage.

She stopped. 'I'm here, child. Where are you?' She inched forward.

The narrow side passageway was filled with the stench of urine – but empty. She waited, trembling and gazing at the light beneath the door at the end of the short hallway. The wind had died momentarily and she stood in the envelope of darkness and floating dust and listened. Small sounds in the night became footsteps, the wind a hissing breath. Every fibre of her wanted to turn and run. But she had heard the child and would not leave.

'God give me strength,' she whispered, and pushed the door open.

The small storeroom was empty. There was an open doorway in front of her that led to another room. But her eyes were not on the second room, they were focused on the light that had drawn her here. Candles burned around a large Nativity scene sitting on the floor, the light casting a wavering glow over a tiny unborn child lying in Christ's manger. The child's eyes were dark holes, the body dried and mummy-like. Without knowing how she knew, she was certain this was Dorothy Regal's missing child. She could not look away from the empty eyes.

Fear was breaking over Sister Ria like sea waves, when she heard the sound of someone running down the alley towards her. She spun around, her fists clenched, and looked into Clemente Rojo's face. Then from the direction of the second room she heard someone or something moving.

She started in the direction of the sound, but Clemente held her back.

'You don't know who's in there,' he said.

'A child is in there,' she said, struggling.

'Listen to me.'

She stopped.

'You stay,' he said, pulling a small silver-plated pistol from his pocket. 'Understand?'

Sister Ria nodded, the pistol surprising her. 'Please hurry.'

Clemente moved past her and disappeared into the second room. She listened to the sound of him walking around, then moving heavy objects that sounded like boxes.

When he returned, the editor looked at her and shook his head, 'Nobody – just an open window and an empty courtyard.'

'No child?' she asked.

He shook his head again.

'We have to find it.'

'I'll look again. You stay put.' He studied her face to make certain she would.

She nodded.

Clemente went back into the second room and Sister

Ria listened: it sounded as though he was going out of a window. She knelt next to the tiny corpse, slowly rocking back and forth on her knees, her hands pressed together in prayer. 'God loves you,' she murmured.

Then a large black moth was fluttering around the flames of the candles, the draughts of heat wafting it up and down over the fires until it banked away, circling and then landing on the shrivelled face of the dead foetus, its wings opening and shutting slowly. She drew in a sharp breath and wondered if the moth was the Antichrist in another form, come to claim the infant's soul. 'Leave in the name of Jesus Christ,' she said. But it did not leave and she struck at it with all her might, causing it to swirl in the backwash of her swing. It climbed the wall, batting its wings as it searched desperately for an escape, then, exhausted, it landed on the dirty plaster.

Sister Ria stood slowly, her eyes locked on the dark creature. '*Get out,*' she mumbled. '*In the name of the Lord, get out!*' She grabbed an old broom lying on the floor and smashed the insect against the wall.

She was on her knees and gazing at the dark smear of the moth's body when Clemente came back. He looked at the side of her face, then at her clenched hands. Her breath was coming in short gasps.

'Sister, are you OK?' he asked, leaning down and studying her features.

Sister Ria struggled to find her voice.

'You OK?' he said again, slipping the small pistol inside his waistcoat.

She nodded and tried to stand but her legs gave way. Clemente caught her.

'The child?'

'I'll keep looking.'

94

Clemente gazed down at the manger. 'Dead for some time,' he said.

She didn't answer, her eyes fixed on the moth.

He looked at her. 'This isn't a good place at night.'

While she liked the man, she wondered what he was doing here at this hour. 'How did you find me?' She thought he took too long to answer.

'I was headed back to my office from the hotel when I heard you calling someone. You sounded frightened.'

The answer sounded right enough and she nodded and knelt and placed a handkerchief over the dead child, praying silently for a few minutes. When she finally stood her legs were still shaky and she stumbled and Clemente caught her shoulders again, steadying her until she was able to pick up the manger and the child.

Clemente reached for the manger. She hesitated and then handed it to him and started out of the door.

That was when she saw it.

Someone was standing in shadows a few yards down the darkened passage. She moved towards the figure.

Immediately, it started off at a loping run.

'Wait!' she yelled. But the figure did not wait. Dressed darkly and moving fast, Sister Ria was having a hard time following the person with her eyes.

'You wait!' she yelled again, increasing her own speed. Whoever it was had turned down a side passage. Seconds later, she reached this same narrow lane.

She slid to a stop.

There was a street lamp at the far end that cast illumination down the passage's full length. She sucked in her breath. Nothing was moving. There were no doors, no windows, no side passages. And there was no one else. The surrounding walls rose fifty feet on either side, the narrow lane dead-ending into another wall. She shuddered and stepped into the passageway.

Something moved. She squinted into the night, following a shadowy beast-like shape as it loped away into the darkness. She trotted after it, slowing to a walk as she neared the end of the passage. Whatever it was had stopped moving. She crept forward, her body shaking. Then she saw it and let her breath out.

'Sister – what are you doing?' Clemente called out to her.

'Nothing,' she said, watching the frightened dog running away. She was still panting hard when Clemente Rojo joined her.

'What's wrong?' he asked.

'Someone was standing in the alley watching us. You saw them.'

Clemente studied her face, 'No, Sister, I didn't.'

She stared down the narrow lane again. 'Well, someone was here.'

'Where did they go?' Clemente asked, still watching her.

The growing frustration she had been feeling for days broke inside her. 'I saw them!' she snapped.

'I'm sure you saw something, Sister.' He paused. 'There's a lot of dust.'

'No – listen to me! I saw a person.' She was suddenly overcome with shame. 'Forgive me. I'm sorry. There's not much light. Maybe I didn't see anyone.' But Sister Ria did not believe that.

Clemente placed the small manger and the infant on the carriage seat and took her elbow and helped her crawl up. She was still shaking. The editor backed the horse out of the narrow passageway, his eyes studying her face. She knew he thought she was a lunatic, hearing voices, seeing people who disappeared, chasing after dogs. He probably thought she had planted the crib and the dead child in the room. She didn't care.

'You don't know who it was you saw?' he asked over the howling wind.

He had tried to sound as if he believed her. She was certain he did not.

Her head was pounding. 'No, I don't.'

She was clucking the carriage horse into a walk when she saw the small man in the brown suit and dark fedora standing on the other side of the street smoking a cigarette and watching her. Then he flicked the cigarette away and started off down the sidewalk towards the hotel. She slapped the reins on the rump of the little grey, steering the animal towards him. Perhaps he had seen the person going in or coming out of the alley.

'Excuse me, sir,' she called.

The man did not stop walking.

'Sir?' she called again, louder.

The man continued walking.

'Sir – please, I'm talking to you!' she yelled.

But the little man ignored her and turned into the front door of the Pico Hotel. Surely he had heard her. She pulled the carriage to a stop and watched him disappear into the crowded lobby. He was the same person she had seen in the marketplace that morning.

Clemente Rojo stood in the centre of the road watching her yelling at the man. Then he started off towards the offices of *La Verdad*. She slapped the reins on the rump of the horse and headed for home at a fast trot.

The hacienda was dark. But Sister Ria needed no light to find the storage room. Her heart was racing. She was feeling with her hands across the top shelf, groping in the darkness for it. She struggled with a match and lit the candle in the wall sconce. She could see the darker rectangle in the paint where the Lugo family crib had sat for years on the shelf. It was gone.

She came out of the room moving fast and did not stop until she was standing in front of her father's bedroom door. She listened. The hallway and the room behind the door were silent. She knocked. There was no response. She wondered why she even bothered and shoved down on the heavy bronze lever, pushing the door in. The room was every bit as dark as the hallway.

'Father.'

Silence.

She moved past the tall candelabrum, touching the wax of the candles. Cold. She yanked the curtains away from the wall. The sheets of his bed were cool to the touch, the top of the stone slab icy. Then she searched through the closets and the two armoires that held his costumes, looking for anything that would make some sense out of the chaos of her mind. Nothing. She wandered around in the dark of the room and began to cry and did not know why.

She stopped in front of a curtain at the rear of the large room and pulled it back and stood looking at a small door. She had seen it before over the years, but she had never seen it open or known what was behind it. She knocked softly. No answer. She tried the handle: locked. She took matches from the side table and was starting to strike one when the bedroom was suddenly filled with lamplight and she turned and faced Aba. The old woman did not look pleased.

'May I help you?' Aba asked, sternly.

98

'My father – where is he?'

'Obviously not in his room. And you should not be either.'

'What is behind this door, Aba?'

'Nothing that belongs to you, child.'

Sister Ria wiped sweat from her face. 'I need to know.'

'Things of the Patrón.'

'What things?'

'Personal.'

'Books?'

'I don't know what you mean.'

'Are there books inside the room? Specifically a book of Tennyson poems?'

Aba studied her face for a moment. 'No.'

Sister Ria leaned close to the door. 'Father, if you are in there –'

'He is not.'

'Then where, Aba?'

'I have no idea, child. It is not my business. Nor yours.'

'The Nativity crib is missing from the closet.'

The old woman shrugged. 'Many things are missing. Los ladrones –'

'I found it in town. There was a dead child in the manger –' she stopped and caught her breath.

'And you blame your father for this?' The old woman paused for a moment, her eyes narrowing. 'You told me you were going to try and save him.'

'No, Aba. I said I would look into Dorothy Regal's death. That's all.'

'And you find these things – and you blame your father.'

Sister Ria didn't know who to blame. But the crib belonged to the Lugo family. And if he had murdered Dorothy Regal and taken her unborn child, it would have

99

been just like him to place the crib and the foetus in the alley as a mad joke. Yes, just like him.

Sister Ria lit a kerosene lamp and moved past Aba back out into the long hallway. She began a search of the house, room by room. Aba followed. They did not speak. When she was convinced that her father was not inside the hacienda, when she had searched every room, looked behind curtains, walked through the large stone cellar, she turned on the old woman.

'Perhaps you believe you are helping him – but you are not.'

'Isadora, your tone,' Aba chided. She paused. 'The Patrón wanders the grounds at night. You are well aware of that. It helps him to think, and then to sleep.'

Sister Ria shook her head and then turned and walked quickly out the door.

'You must slow down, child.'

Sister Ria whirled around. 'Where is he?'

'Do not speak to me in that manner, Isadora.' Aba studied her face. 'I could not tell you where the Patrón has gone.'

Sister Ria went out into the darkness. She searched the gardens and work sheds, then moved slowly through the huge equestrian barn, the horses sticking their heads out of their stalls and watching her. When she had not found her father, she headed back to the Lugo family chapel and the dead child she had placed on God's altar.

Don Maximiato Rialto Lugo, tiny in stature and wiry thin, looked like a small boy playing at being a Catholic priest. He was standing before the altar in purple vestments, a white satin sash around his narrow waist, his arms thrown wide in an urgent appeal to the heavens, then he turned and swung a filigreed silver ball on a long chain, dispensing clouds of sharp-smelling incense through the shadowy air. Candles burned on both sides of the altar.

Sister Ria stopped at the edge of the front pew and genuflected, doubts clouding her mind. She had not expected to find him here. If Aba was right – that he had simply been wandering the grounds this night – then Milagros could be right.

'Father, where have you been?'

He was speaking in Latin verses.

'Father?'

'Have you no respect?'

'You are not a priest.'

'I can –' was all he said.

'Father, listen to me.'

He was mumbling something.

'I will have a priest come in the morning for the child.'

'No priest.'

'Yes. The child must be blessed and buried with her mother.' She watched him for a moment. 'Where were you tonight?'

He turned and looked down from the altar at her, intensely focused, like the white herons that stalked fish in the sea marshes. He was sweating in the cool air. Always he had been a difficult man – unstable, cross-grained, cynical, a scoffer; but now she sensed that he was insane.

'I have adventures with God,' he said.

'Father, you are not well.'

He waved her away with his hand. 'I sleep in the arms of saints.'

'You sleep in drugged stupors.'

He tilted his head and appeared to be listening to a sound in the darkness that she could not hear. 'There is something mysterious to my life,' he said, turning back to the altar. When he turned around again he was holding the tiny corpse in his hands.

'Put the child down, Father.'

He ignored her and stepped into the circle of candle-light and dipped a hand into the font, dripping water over the shrivelled body.

'I baptize you in the name of the Father –'

Sister Ria was not hearing the words. She was staring at the bottom edge of his vestments, opening and shut-ting her mouth in small gasps. He was wearing riding boots and spurs beneath his robes. She jerked her head up, her eyes narrowing. 'You were in that alley – in that room. You were there, weren't you?'

'– the Son –'

'Answer me!'

The cavernous equestrian barn was dimly lit by dozens of lanterns, the soft light wavering against stone reminding her of the convent. Sister Ria was darting in and out of the stalls, startling horses as she went. Auel, the old barn master, trotted behind her, hat in hand, looking worried.

'Auel, I am not checking your work,' she said, walking quickly past the little man.

Six stalls later, she found what she was searching for. She yanked the blanket off the back of a small black mare, the little horse twitching and jittery, her eyes rolling to white at this woman in her black robes who stood running her hand over the damp rectangular saddle mark on her back. Sister Ria gazed blindly at the stable wall, as if she had suddenly forgotten what she was doing.

Finally, she said, 'Who rode this animal tonight?'

'She is the Patrón's.'

102

Sister Ria turned and was walking quickly towards the huge door of the barn when she saw a shadow on the wall stir. 'Auel, who else is in here?'

'I allow no one but the Patrón and you, Señora. I do not allow it.'

'Father?' she called.

There was no response.

'No one, Señora.'

She stood watching the shadows. 'Yes, I saw someone.'

'Possums hunt the young pigeons.'

'No,' she said, her eyes searching the huge barn.

Auel took a lantern off the wall and turned the wick up; the flame rose and cast a wide circle of yellow light. He marched off down the hallway in search of phantoms and ghosts, muttering to himself. Sister Ria followed. He was right: they found no one.

But Sister Ria had seen the shadow.

The Patrón was no longer in the chapel. Sister Ria ran down the dark service road, through the courtyard and into the rear of the hacienda, moving down the loggia quickly towards his room. Her eyes were adjusting to the deeper darkness inside the house when Aba suddenly loomed in the shadows in front of her, leaning with both hands on her cane.

'Why are you doing this, child?'

There was a chair next to the wall. The old woman had been waiting for her, Sister Ria realized. Her anger grew.

'Where is he?'

'Dressing for bed. And you will not bother him.'

'Yes, I shall bother him!' Sister Ria cried. 'I did what I said I would: I looked into Dorothy Regal's murder . . .

and I know now that he killed her. He is a murderer. Do you understand, Aba?'

'Do not speak such things.'

'He murdered that girl and her unborn child.' Sister Ria was rushing her words.

'I have asked you –'

'No, no, no, you can't protect him! He killed that –'

The slap was fast and hard, jerking Sister Ria's head to the side, silencing her as if the words had been knocked from her mouth. Then slowly she began to sob, her body heaving with each surge of breath.

When she was finally able to control herself, she wiped her eyes on the sleeve of her habit and looked at the old servant. Aba was staring at the floor.

'Why have you stayed with him all these years? Why, Aba?'

'Forgive me, child. I had no right –'

'Why, Aba? Why have you stayed?'

The woman just shook her head. 'Forgive me.'

'I forgive you. Now tell me why.'

The old servant turned and began walking down the hallway.

Sister Ria watched her until she found her voice and said, 'You love him.'

Aba did not answer.

'Aba?'

The woman continued down the hall, disappearing into the shadows.

Sister Ria was slowly rubbing the tips of her fingers over the tiny face of Jesus on the small golden crucifix her mother had given her as a child. She was sitting in a chair in the darkness of her room, thinking about her life, about things lost, wondering how Aba could love him.

She shook her head. It didn't matter how. All that mattered was that this old woman who had raised her, nurtured her, protected her – this woman she loved deeply – loved him. And because of that, Sister Ria would not condemn him out of hand. Not without proof.

She loved Aba far too much to do less.

Fernando leaped up on the bed and sat down and she felt comforted by his presence. She wanted to reach out to touch him. But she knew better.

SIX DAYS . . .

TEN

There were seven of them silently lined up in the pre-dawn darkness of the hacienda's loggia, just outside the Patrón's bedroom. It looked like the makings of a police raid. Sister Ria had organized it as soon as Aba had left with Valla, the cook, for the morning shopping in the marketplace. The women would not be back for some three hours.

Min was standing at the head of the line, looking sick to his stomach. Sister Ria stepped up to him and said, 'Key, please.'

He looked even sicker.

'Min, give me the key.'

The boy fished a ring of keys from his gown and reluctantly handed them over.

'Thank you,' she said, knocking on the heavy door. When there was the standard silence, she said, 'Father, we are coming in.' Then she turned to the line of servants, Min and two other male servants and four cleaning maids, and said, 'Do not falter. He will yell, he will threaten, but you must do your duty. Is that understood?'

They all looked pale now as if they had just been given

an order to stop a charge of Russian Cossacks with their mops and brooms. Several of them nodded nervously.

'Good. Pick up your equipment.' She turned the key and shoved the door open.

It was the first time in her life that she had ever seen the Patrón surprised. He was lying under his covers, glasses on his nose, propped up on pillows and sketching on a pad, smugly confident his door was locked. His mouth dropped open.

For a long moment no one said anything or moved. Then Don Maximiato yelled, 'Aba!' as if he was being attacked by savages.

'She is at the market,' Sister Ria said, waving the line of servants inside, 'and we have come to clean your room.'

'You will not!'

'You can stay in your bed and we will clean around you. Or you can leave.'

'You insolent child!' he shouted.

'It is for your own good. The room is filthy and not healthy,' she explained, knowing that was not the reason. She had come to search for the book of poems. The day before, she had hurriedly looked for it while he was painting in the garden and had not found it. This time she would take the room apart shelf by shelf, drawer by drawer, cover by cover.

Don Maximiato had gone back to sketching on his pad, ignoring them, while the servants stood staring down at him, looking as if they were about to bolt the room.

'Take all of the animals out to the barn so they can be cared for properly. Then I want the flowers thrown away and all of these baskets of food removed to the kitchen for the cooks to look over.' She was pacing back and forth through the maze of crates and baskets, as she had daily

110

walked through the overcrowded wards of the lepers, giving orders and instructions to the Indian orderlies. Fernando followed close behind her looking as though he had just assumed the role of second in command. 'Then the closets and chests are to be emptied and the contents taken out onto the veranda to air. Understood?'

No one moved, their eyes locked on the old Patrón.

'Is that understood?' She clapped her hands and the spell was broken and the work began.

An hour later the room was almost empty and Sister Ria was going through the drawers of a tall chest that stood across the room from her father's bed. They had not spoken during the entire procedure. The Patrón had remained in bed sketching madly and talking to himself.

He looked up at her and pulled off his glasses. 'Do you find sin confusing?'

'No, Father, I don't.'

'I think God got it backwards. Sin is good, avoiding it is bad.'

She ignored him.

'Making love, for example –'

She whirled and faced him. 'Do not dare to talk of such things in front of these young women.'

'Is that a sin – to talk about love? It isn't called making hate.'

She ignored him again and went back to searching the drawers.

'Do you dread Hell?'

'Must you prattle on so?'

'Do you fear death?'

She was humming softly to herself.

'Do you take showers in your robe?'

She turned and looked down at him. 'No, Father, I do

not. Please get out of your bed so that we can change it.'

'I've heard that.'

'What, Father?'

'That nuns shower in their robes.'

'That's ridiculous. Why would they do that?' she said, testily.

'So God does not peek.'

The servants giggled.

'That is enough. Get out of the bed.'

'No – you get out of my room.'

She pursed her lips. 'If you do not get out of the bed, we will take it apart while you are still in it.'

In response, the Patrón suddenly disappeared beneath the covers, thrashing and scurrying about.

'What, pray tell, are you doing, Father?'

He mumbled something but she could not make out the words. Moments later, his head popped out of the covers again.

'There,' he said, sounding smugly satisfied.

'There what, sir?'

'There, I am naked – so go ahead and take the covers off.' The servants froze.

'Entirely naked,' he piped.

Sister Ria looked at him for a time and then said, 'Rosita, Maria, Fabia and Dolores, please leave the room.'

'Totally, absolutely naked.'

They had stripped the bed a quarter of an hour ago and the Patrón had been standing and looking like a plucked chicken in a corner of the room ever since. Twice, Sister Ria had offered him a robe, but both times he had petulantly refused. She was watching Min and the other male servants turning the mattress. The book was not in the room. The only possible place left was the side room.

'Father, where is the key to the side room?'

Once again, as he had been doing periodically since he had been forced from the bed, he bent over and put his hands on his bony knees and aimed his posterior at Sister Ria. Min and the other male servants began to giggle.

'Silencio!' she snapped.

Her father straightened up.

'Thank you for your cooperation,' she said. 'I will find the key later. Min, please make up the Patrón's bed, before he catches pneumonia.' Sister Ria turned and started for the door.

'Nun, I have a gift for you,' he said, tearing a page from his sketch pad.

She turned back and took the offered paper. It was a drawing of her, stark naked and taking a shower, a large crucifix dangling between her breasts . . . and through a nearby window peeked a bearded old man with leering eyes who she knew could only be God.

Sister Ria tore the paper into small pieces and tossed them on the floor.

'I thought you had come to clean my room,' he chirped.

ELEVEN

Mist from the sea was rising up the canyons, mixing with the morning sunlight and spreading a red hue over the hacienda's kitchen, when Sister Ria entered. She was exhausted, a worrisome frustration building in her chest. They hadn't found the book and she didn't know what to do next. Aba had returned from the market an hour earlier and had quickly organized the reassembly of the Patrón's bedroom. She was not happy. The old woman watched her now as if she were still a child. Sister Ria avoided her gaze and sat in a chair at the opposite end of the long kitchen table. She took a steaming cup of Mexican coffee from a silver tray held by a young servant girl. 'Gracias,' she said.

The girl curtseyed and then stood looking at Sister Ria. She was perhaps fifteen or sixteen.

'What is your name, child?'

'Cristina, Señora,' the girl said.

'It is nice to meet you, Cristina.'

The girl looked suddenly anxious.

'Child?'

114

'May I speak with you?' she whispered.

Aba looked up from her seat at the far end of the table. 'Cristina,' she said, her voice sharp. 'You know better than to bother the Señora.'

'She isn't, Aba,' Sister Ria said, and to Cristina, 'Certainly.'

The old woman ignored her and pointed at a broom leaning against a wall and the girl set down the silver tray and hurried over to it. 'Perhaps not – but she will behave properly.' The old servant's chin elevated slightly. 'There are proper ways to behave in this life, Isadora.'

'The room needed cleaning.'

Aba, ever mindful of her role as head servant, did not continue the discussion in front of the staff. She looked instead to a small alcove at the far end of the kitchen and suddenly clapped her hands.

'To work!' she snapped.

Sister Ria turned and jumped. There were fifteen or sixteen children seated on reed mats around a small mountain of red peppers, sitting so quietly that she had not noticed them in the kitchen's bustling activities. Some no older than five or six, their small hands running heavy needles and string through the pepper pods so they could be hung to dry like bright red and yellow necklaces on the adobe walls. The children were barefoot and in rags.

She stood and walked over and smiled down at them.

'Buenos Dias, niños,' she said.

The children looked nervously at Aba.

'Street orphans,' Aba called. 'Sullen.'

'No, God's special children,' Sister Ria said, smiling down at them. The children smiled back. She ruffled the hair of a small copper-headed girl of four or five and returned to the table and her coffee.

115

'The Patrón feeds them,' Aba said.

'They do not look fed, Aba.'

'I make them work first.' Aba had risen and was standing at the table's edge between the two housemaids, a starched black apron over her stark white blouse, a black lace cap on her head, watching as the women polished the dining ware.

'Please feed them now, Aba,' Sister Ria said, her thoughts leaping to the orphan children of Poona.

Aba was staring down silently at the table top.

'Aba?'

Sister Ria's eyes locked on the oldest among them, an Indian girl of twelve or thirteen, pretty, tall and thin, with a sweet grace to her movements. But she was filthy and too far into her womanhood to be wearing paper-thin rags such as her blouse.

'Aba? Did you hear?'

The old servant looked up from the silver cleaning and watched Sister Ria for a moment before she called out in a husky voice, 'Valla, prepare the meal.'

'Thank you,' Sister Ria said, returning to her coffee and the telegram that had come for her the night before: '*Santa Osita. See Governor – two days. Nothing you can do. Leave. Millie.*' Hope surged in her that Millie would be able to stay the madness – and she brought her hands, palms pressed together, to her face and whispered a prayer for her sister, her lips moving silently.

Finished, Sister Ria sat half-listening to the idle chatter of the servants as they went back to their work, the voices recalling to mind her Sisters in India. She missed them, their love and companionship. She even missed the never-ending litany of nursing and feeding and consoling, cleaning the great corridors and huge high rooms, scrubbing the stones, washing the filthy bedding and clothing of the sick and dying. They were constantly exhausted by the drudgery but never able to quit because the tasks were never done and God would never be satisfied until they were. Sister Ria noticed the oldest of the orphan girls watching her. 'Come here, child,' she said.

The girl looked nervously at Aba.

'The Doña has asked you to come – so come.'

The girl stood quickly, as if she had been shocked, and walked in a scuttling motion towards Sister Ria, dragging one of her feet as if it were a bag of sand.

Watching her move, Sister Ria realized the girl was even lovelier than she had first thought, tall and beautifully graceful even with the deformity. The girl stopped in front of her, gazing awkwardly at the floor. Sister Ria looked down at the child's shoes: men's brogans, badly scuffed and broken down, one of them cut open so the twisted foot could be inserted.

'What is your name?'

'Estrella, Sister,' she said, still studying the floor.

Sister Ria smiled. 'Look up at me, please.'

Slowly the girl raised her face.

Sister Ria examined her features carefully before she said, 'Yes, I thought so. You are indeed one of God's stars in Heaven.'

The girl's face brightened some, but she did not smile.

'How old are you, Estrella?'

The girl was looking back down at her shoes. 'I don't know, Sister.'

The child's embarrassment reminded her of her own childhood and she pressed her lips together against the sadness and forced herself to laugh. 'What a wonderful thing for a woman to be able to honestly say.' Sister Ria

117

turned to Aba. The old woman was looking displeased by these unscheduled interruptions to the work of pepper stringing. 'Aba, please have the maids prepare a bath in my room.'

'Now? At mid-morning?'

'Yes, please, now.' And to Estrella, she said, 'Come with me.'

Sister Ria was starting for the door when her father came marching into the kitchen followed quickly by Min and two young Indian servant boys. All were carrying armfuls of brightly coloured toy drums, horns and whistles that they began to distribute to the laughing children. Don Lugo was dressed in a band leader's uniform with a blue ostrich plume stuck on top of his tall white hat. He looked like a little organ-grinder's monkey, she thought.

'Fall in,' he yelled.

Sister Ria watched him in disbelief. Six days from his own execution and he was playing foolish games with children. Surely he was mad.

The children were banging and blowing on their new toys, the noise deafening. Aba looked angry – the Patrón, gleeful.

'Don Lugo,' the old servant said over the din, 'the pepper stringing.'

'Fudge the pepper stringing. La musica! Line up – line up!'

The children had obviously played this game before and quickly lined up in ranks of two, forming a long uneven queue in the kitchen.

'Father,' Sister Ria said.

He did not respond but instead moved a sad-looking fat boy with a bad case of mange to the lofty position at the head of the line, patting the boy's shoulder. 'Beat your drum loudly, niño – we will march to the sound of it. Shoulders back, chin up!' The boy looked suddenly proud.

'Father!' she repeated.

He held up his hand to the children. 'Atención, musicos!' he shouted, and the noise stopped. He turned and looked at Sister Ria. Then he looked at Estrella, noticing her awkward stance, his eyes moving down to her misshapen foot.

Sister Ria tried to stop him, 'Father, do not –'

He ignored her, pursing his lips as if in deep thought. 'You have a splay foot – no, actually it is a club foot.'

Sister Ria could see the embarrassment on the girl's face.

'Father, please –' Sister Ria whispered.

'Be quiet. It is not your foot.' Then he stopped and looked up at Min. 'Do we have enough instruments?' he asked, as if this was very important.

The boy nodded. The man examined the misshapen foot.

'The children need shoes before they need toys.' Sister Ria said. 'Even you must understand –'

'Isadora,' Aba said firmly.

Don Lugo held up his hand again, this time to silence the old servant, his eyes on Sister Ria, while he put the shoe back on Estrella's twisted foot. He was smiling at Sister Ria. Or maybe it was a sneer. The children were standing at attention in their long line, fingering their new toys and nervously watching the two of them. Fernando leaped down from the chair and watched as well, seemingly hopeful that a fight might be breaking out. He loved a good fight.

For a brief moment, Sister Ria thought that her father might actually agree with her. Then Don Lugo patted Estrella's shoe and let it go and filled his lungs with air and shouted, 'La musica!' and the children began to play a mad collection of discordant notes and banging sounds, until she wanted to cover her ears. Then they were marching in ragged order out the door, Don Lugo high stepping like the band leader of an insane asylum. Fernando, his tail stuck high in the air, followed smartly behind, looking as if he thought this crowd a lot more interesting than the head servant and the nun.

Sister Ria was pacing her steps to the hobbling gait of Estrella, the two of them headed down the long hallway towards her bedroom, when Cristina suddenly stepped out in front of them. 'Good Sister,' she hissed, her eyes darting nervously down the loggia towards the kitchen passage. The children's music making had stopped.

'Yes, Cristina?'

'Last night I heard you tell Señora Aba that the crib of the family was missing.' She gulped some air. 'And that you found a dead child in the manger.'

'Yes?'

The girl hesitated.

'Go ahead, child. Nothing will happen to you.'

'I saw the Patrón walking with it near the old work sheds.'

'When?'

'This was after we had cleaned the blood from your room.' The girl lowered her head and looked embarrassed. 'I was with my boyfriend in the loft of the stable.'

'Yes?'

'I heard someone outside and looked down and saw the Patrón walking towards the work sheds carrying the crib. It was very late –'

'Are you sure it was the Patrón?'

120

Cristina nodded. 'It was dark, but I could see. He was wearing his gaucho hat and a black cape that I have seen him in.'

'Cristina,' Aba snapped. The old woman was approaching down the hallway from the kitchen. 'I have already told you once this morning not to bother the Doña.'

'Thank you, Aba, but it is I who bothered Cristina.' Sister Ria turned and nodded at the young girl. 'Thank you, Cristina. You may go about your work now.'

'Yes,' Aba said, 'your work.'

The girl hurried away.

In the distance the children's mad music could be heard again, her father shouting, 'Right . . . Left . . . Square those lines . . . About face!' something wildly joyous in the sound, but not to Sister Ria, not at this moment. Estrella had dried off from the bath and was behind the dressing screen trying on clothes while Sister Ria stood before the open doors of a large armoire pulling out more clothes. Aba watched her, looking as if she had fingers drumming inside her head, holding a beautiful black silk scarf that she had removed from the armoire. The same scarf that Isadora had used to cover herself with during Mass. But Sister Ria's thoughts were not on clothing or scarves – she was thinking about what Cristina had told her.

'The dresses were purchased for you, by your mother,' Aba said.

'And never worn.'

'And should not be worn by –'

Sister Ria looked quickly at her and something in her eyes caused Aba to hesitate. When the old woman finally

121

continued, she said only, 'by anyone.' Then she turned away and searched through the small jewellery box on top of the chest of drawers, removing a large red garnet clasp that Isadora had used to clamp the scarf under her chin.

'I wish only to remind you,' Aba continued, 'that you are the daughter of the Patrón. That you have responsibilities.' She laid the scarf and the red brooch down on top of the chest and began to tap a foot against the tile floor.

Sister Ria watched her a moment, 'May I speak to you in the hall, Aba?'

The servant tipped her head slightly. 'Of course.'

Outside in the loggia, Sister Ria looked out the window at the morning mist burning off the distant fields in the sunlight, Aba standing behind her. Without turning, she said, 'He was seen carrying the crib from the house. The crib I found the dead child in, Aba.'

'Is that something Cristina has said?'

'It doesn't matter who said it. He took the crib from the house and I found the dead child in it.'

'The girl is becoming bothersome.'

'It doesn't matter who said it. It happened.'

'I say the Patrón did not do these things. I have told you that before.'

Sister Ria turned and studied Aba's face for a long time before she nodded and started back into the bedroom. Aba grabbed her arm and turned her around.

'No, you will not walk away. I raised you, Isadora Victorine, and you will hear me out,' Aba snapped. 'You have stood against your father for too many years. He is going to be executed. It is time you put away what was done. If you don't, child, you will end up hating yourself for hating him.'

'This has nothing to do with me.'

Aba was trembling now. 'Do not tell me a lie, Isadora!' she hissed, looking to see that none of the servants or the young girl in the bedroom were listening. 'I will leave this house before I will allow that.'

Sister Ria remained at the window for a long time listening to the faint sound of the children's wild music. It didn't matter what she felt about him, there were only six days of life left for him and she didn't know if he was guilty. And she had to know. She could hear Aba talking in the bedroom behind her, the woman's tone was once again that of the head servant. She reached and lifted the latch to the bedroom.

Aba nodded respectfully as she came through the door.

Estrella looked beautiful with her lovely pale, unblemished skin, her cheeks glowing from the hot bath, her thick brown hair casually pulled up in a bunch to the top of her head and tied with a yellow ribbon, her face a thing of beauty. Estrella was wearing a simple yellow dress, collared and belted at the waist. She was looking down at the fine linen material as though it might suddenly disappear if she looked away.

Aba motioned for her to turn in a circle. When this was done, Aba walked over to the chest, running her hands over the top. She turned and looked at Sister Ria. 'I laid the scarf and brooch here –'

Sister Ria nodded.

'They are not here.' The old woman turned to Estrella. 'Did you take them?'

Estrella shook her head. 'No, Señora. I would not have done such a thing.'

'Of course you wouldn't,' Sister Ria said, pulling back from her thoughts. 'It's probably just one of the younger servants playing a joke.'

'The servants do not do such things in this house, Señora,' Aba said, still staring at Estrella. Estrella shook her head.

The door to the central garden was open and Sister Ria stepped out into the sunshine. No one was there, and she returned to the bedroom. 'Estrella, take the dress off so that it can be altered, and put on the blue one. It will do for now. Aba will find everyday things for you to wear.'

Sister Ria waited until the girl had disappeared behind the screen before she turned to the old woman. 'I'm sure the brooch and scarf will show up.'

'The girl is a thief.'

'She is not a thief, Aba,' Sister Ria whispered.

'Do you see them?'

Sister Ria glanced around the room. 'They have been misplaced, that's all. But it doesn't matter, Aba.'

The old woman stared at the tile floor for a moment and then looked up at Sister Ria and said, 'They are your things, Isadora.'

Sister Ria nodded. 'Please have Min put a bed in this room for the child. She is too old to sleep unprotected at night. And please find work for her in the house.'

'You are now the Doña of the hacienda,' Aba said, as if this would bring a halt to Sister Ria's madness.

'No. I am God's servant, Aba.'

The old woman gazed at Sister Ria for a moment, then tipped her head. 'As you direct.'

Min had brought her the news of the young messenger's arrival moments before and was bowing in front of her.

'Min, do not keep doing that. Please.' The teenage servant stood up and smiled and walked quickly down the hallway towards the boy.

Sister Ria followed him. The boy looked as if he had run all the way. He was a young Mexican of twelve or thirteen, thin, barefoot, his rough clothing damp with sweat. Min tipped his head towards Sister Ria and the boy trotted quickly down the hallway towards her. As he approached, he took off his hat and stood with bowed head until Sister Ria asked him to stand up.

She smiled. 'Who are you?'

'Francisco, Sister. I have been sent by Monsignor Abel.' He stopped and cleared his throat.

'It is a pleasure to meet you, Francisco,' she said, pouring him a glass of water from a pewter pitcher that sat on a nearby table.

He drank the water down without stopping for air.

'Gracias, Sister,' he panted, smiling. Then the smile left his face. 'The Monsignor wants you to know that he cannot do as you wish.'

'Is the Monsignor ill?' Sister Ria asked.

'Not when I left him, Sister. He was eating his breakfast and looked fine. He said only that your father had committed mortal sin and that the child and her mother also died in sin.' Francisco had pulled himself up straight and stiffly delivered the message with the full force and gravity of his office as messenger for the Catholic prelate of Los Angeles.

Sister Ria bit at her lip and then turned to Aba. 'Please see that Francisco has something to eat and then is driven back to town.'

'Gracias,' the boy said. 'Do you have a message for the Monsignor?' he asked.

Sister Ria shook her head.

Aba turned her thin shoulders to the young messenger, her expression hawk-like, and said, 'Yes. The Lugo family has a message for the grand personage. Tell him that we did not expect him to come – our invitation was merely a formality, a simple courtesy. Extended and now withdrawn. I will have it written out so that the Monsignor receives it all. Every word.' She looked at Min. He started to bow but caught himself and stood straight. Aba glared at him. He bowed. She nodded.

When Sister Ria next saw her father he had abandoned his role as the leader of the children's marching band and was now dressed in the bright orange robes of a Tibetan monk, his head covered with a Sherpa's goatskin skullcap. He was standing in a large sandy circle behind the gardens, rocking back and forth on his spindly legs, crouched and high stepping like a skinny Sumo wrestler, holding a long hickory stave in his hands. A dozen Mexican workers lined the edge of the circle, while one of their own was dressed in an awkward-looking suit of padded straw resembling a fat scarecrow. The man was wearing one of her father's medieval jousting helmets and holding his own heavy hickory stick.

Twice the size of the Patrón, the man was smiling confidently out from his raised visor, shoving his staff in front of him as if pushing back invisible opponents and grunting loudly. The men standing around the circle were nodding and elbowing one another. The Patrón ignored them all, high stepping still, then slamming his long stick down on the earth as though he were killing snakes, chanting in a language she had never heard before. Min was standing stiffly to one side of Don Maximiato, holding a large silver

126

tray with a glass and a pitcher of water on it, a white towel over his arm. The boy bowed when he saw Sister Ria approaching.

'Stop that, please, Min,' she snapped, her patience wearing thin.

The boy stood and grinned.

Fernando was sitting at the side of the dirt circle looking as if he was thoroughly enjoying himself.

'Father, I need to talk with you,' Sister Ria called from the edge of the circle. The workers were pulling off their hats and crossing themselves at the sight of her. She blessed them with the sign and then turned back to her father. As she did, the big man in the straw suit pulled off his heavy helmet and stood with his head respectfully bowed. 'Bless you, sir, but I would defend myself at all times against this man.'

The caution came too late.

Her father had suddenly stopped high stepping and raised his staff over his head with both hands and yelled, 'Eiieeee!' attacking the man, who was fortunate enough to get his helmet back on his head before the first blow struck. He staggered forward and then began swinging wildly at the leaping figure of her father. The men were cheering. Fernando was clicking his teeth, his one eye glued on the battle.

Sister Ria shook her head and stomped back to the hacienda.

TWELVE

The window was open in Dr Reed Johnson's office and Sister Ria was sitting in a stiff wooden chair in a medical smock, gazing out at the street and wondering how a priest could believe it possible for an unborn to die in sin and refuse to hear the confession of a condemned man? It seemed so wrong. Surely Monsignor Abel had misunderstood. She would talk with him.

Even in the growing morning heat her bare head felt cool without the veil, and she ran her hands repeatedly through her short hair, mulling the jumbled happenings of the past few days over and over in her mind. 'I'm trying, Mother,' Sister Ria sighed.

Dr Johnson cleared his throat. 'Isadora?' The man was perched on a stool writing something at his desk in front of her, the listening tube hanging from his neck, tapping quietly against the wood as he worked.

'Nothing, Doctor,' she said.

Small and bald, somewhere in his seventies, Reed Johnson had been the Lugo family physician all her life. His office was on the fourth floor of a building on the west side of Main Street, and across the wide boulevard Sister Ria could see a solid wall of taller buildings and hear the discordant noise of heavy street traffic and the sound of construction.

Then her eyes locked on the imposing red stone edifice that housed the Los Angeles Gas Company – the offices of L. Summerville and Samuel Atkins – standing two blocks away, looking stately in the morning sun. She had been avoiding that building. She knew she had to talk to the men, but about what, she had no idea. She couldn't just march inside and ask them if they had murdered Dorothy Regal. She had no evidence, just Milagros' suspicions. And Milagros had said they were dangerous men.

Dr Johnson turned on the stool and faced her.

'You can get dressed now,' he said, nodding towards the canvas screen in the corner of the room. He went back to working on the papers strewn over his desk. A few minutes later, he said, 'Having worked in hospitals with this disease, I assume you know the health laws that most countries follow regarding it, Isadora: you are to be locked away in quarantine for two years if you show any sign of it.'

'Yes –' she said from behind the screen.

'You could have hidden the fact of your exposure.'

'No, I couldn't,' she said. 'I had given my word to the Indian officials.'

Johnson smiled as if she had said something humorous. 'I see no sign of any disease.'

She stepped out into the office and adjusted her veil.

The man studied her face. 'How are you?'

She did not respond.

'You seem well.'

Sister Ria walked to the window and looked down at

the street below. Johnson watched her for a moment, then said, 'Close the door on it, Isadora.'

She took a deep breath. 'I don't know what door to close.'

The man was talking, but Sister Ria wasn't hearing. She was listening instead to the faint echoes of her life spent here in this place. When she finally spoke, her voice was barely audible. 'At the convent hospital I saw men who had murdered or molested their own children. And I could still find pity in my heart for them, could feel God's compassion for them. But I can't for my own father. He did nothing physically to me – yet I hate him. And I can't stop.'

She turned from the window and stared through Johnson, as if she was peering into a dark window to Hell. 'He harmed me because he didn't care – not what people thought of me, how badly I was humiliated, not how my life was being destroyed. He simply didn't care. It was as if I didn't exist.' She focused on the man. 'All I ever wanted was to mean something to him. That's all I ever wanted.'

She wiped dampness from her cheeks and drew in her breath. 'In all of my life, he has never once called me his daughter. Not once.'

Johnson nodded his head in sympathy.

She was pulling at her hands, tears streaming down her cheeks. 'I am a nun – and I'm rotting inside with hatred.'

Johnson cleared his throat and said, 'In his way, he –'

She held up her hands and shoved at the air, as if she was shoving the man back, and shook her head hard. 'Please don't. I don't want to hear about his so-called love. Because it never existed.'

*   *   *

The tiny brown adobe dwelling was wedged between two towering brick buildings, a Mexican holdout against the Anglo sprawl of new Los Angeles. Sister Ria did not know where else to go. She had prayed to God and nothing had come to her. She continued walking – being led by a pretty girl of seventeen or eighteen through the small cottage garden in front of the house, the garden filled with pink, red and crimson hollyhocks and a carefully tended patch of medicinal plants: *Yerba Santa,* which the Indians used as a cure for asthma and pneumonia; Poison Toloache, to induce dreams and visions; Death Camas, for boils and rattlesnake bites. There were others she did not recognize. She suddenly wanted to leave. But she could not. She had to have answers.

The girl, who called herself Ofelia, smiled at her and knocked on the sagging wooden front door of the primitive mud house. When there was no response, Ofelia, who said she was the great-great-great-granddaughter of the curandera, Nachita, pushed the door open and motioned Sister Ria into the dark one-room adobe.

Sister Ria stood in the shadows of the ancient house breathing in the smells of a hundred years of smoke and burning herbs and joss sticks, letting her eyes adjust to the dark. The curandera was sitting in a worn armchair in a corner of the room. The fireplace was blazing, even though the morning heat outside was close to 90 degrees. Sister Ria felt a thin sheen of sweat break over her body.

'Grandmother is never warm these days,' Ofelia said, removing the shawl from her shoulders. 'Is that not right, Grandmother?'

The old woman stirred like some sort of hibernating animal. Sister Ria's eyes had dilated to the point where she could see the shrunken figure clearly – her shoulders

131

draped with a heavy black shawl, a dark bandana tied over her head of thin wispy white hair. She had a shaking palsy in her right hand. The face looked like a dried apple core, the eyes lost in slits of sagging skin.

'How old is *Abuela*?' Sister Ria asked the girl.

'One hundred and fifty years,' Ofelia said proudly.

That was impossible, Sister Ria told herself.

'What have you to ask of my grandmother?' the girl said.

'A woman was murdered two months ago, not far from this house. Her name was Dorothy Regal. Abuela, do you know her?'

The old woman neither moved nor spoke.

'Grandmother charges a fee for her services.' Sister Ria placed a gold coin on the table next to the old woman.

'I know no Dorothy Regal,' the old woman wheezed. 'I know a whore.'

'Yes, that was her.'

Ofelia nodded in agreement.

The old woman shrugged. 'If you say.'

'Did she come to see you?' Sister Ria asked.

The old woman nodded.

'What did she want from you, Abuela?'

'To be out of danger.'

'What danger?'

The old woman appeared to drift off into slumber. The granddaughter looked at Sister Ria and said, 'The woman was afraid.'

'Of?'

'Someone had been following her. She was afraid of what they were going to do to her.'

'Did she say who was following her?'

The old woman was snoring softly. Ofelia shook her head. 'No. Just that she was being watched and she wanted grandmother to prepare a potion to protect her.'

'It did not save her,' Sister Ria murmured.

'Grandmother did not prepare it. The woman would not pay.'

'I found a piece of paper in her room with the words: *Brown cutaway.*'

The girl nodded again. 'Yes, I remember that is what Grandmother told her that she read in the smoke.'

'What does it mean?' Sister Ria asked.

'Grandmother?' Ofelia said.

The old woman tipped her head towards the girl. 'What do the words *Brown cutaway* mean? You told the whore those words.'

The old woman sat for a time and then just shrugged.

'She often doesn't know the meaning of what she reads in the smoke.'

Sister Ria pulled herself to her full height and braced herself. 'I have a question, Abuela.'

'You want her to read the smoke?' the girl said.

'Whatever she does, yes.'

'There is a separate charge for this reading.'

Sister Ria placed another coin on the table. Ofelia scooped some coals from the burning fireplace with a small iron shovel and poured them into a heavy metal crock in the centre of the table. Then she helped the old woman pull her chair close and guided her gnarled hands into the rising columns of smoke. Sister Ria's eyes were burning.

'What do you ask her?' the girl said.

Sister Ria hesitated, then cleared the smoke from her throat and in a quiet voice said, 'Did my father murder Dorothy Regal?'

Ofelia did not appear startled by the question and Sister Ria guessed that the young girl had heard hundreds of ugly secrets in this dark room.

They waited. The old woman said nothing.

Ofelia whispered something into her ear but she just sat, her withered hands blackening slowly in the smoke. Then Nachita shook her head in response.

'I'm sorry. Grandmother sees nothing.'

Sister Ria was turning to leave, when the old woman began to flex her fingers in the rising wisps, grasping at strands of the grey vapour as if trying to catch things inside it. 'The boy,' she murmured.

'The child I heard in the alley?'

The old woman shrugged.

'I don't understand.'

Nachita shook her head, annoyed by the distraction, and milked the smoke with her hands again. Then she took a sudden deep breath and spat out the words, 'Dragged to death,' as if they were bitter.

Sister Ria brought her hands – palms pressed together – to her face, her thoughts flying backwards in time to the summer of her sixteenth year.

She had hidden in her bedroom the evening he came calling. Ruperto Tristán was from Mexico City, seventeen years old, worldly and handsome. He was spending the summer with his aunt's family, the Valdez, wealthy Los Angeles merchants, and he had taken to Isadora, as if her masculine clothing only enhanced her charms. Unlike Milagros and the other well-bred girls of the pueblo, she had not been chaperoned, but rather left by her father to do as she wished, and she and Ruperto had spoken a number of times on the streets. Once they had even walked boldly through the plaza gardens together, touching hands, her young heart speeding with joy.

Still, the night he came calling she had panicked and hidden in her room. Young men came courting Milagros all the time. But none had ever come to see her. They were forbidden by their families to have anything to do with her – this half-man-girl who worked in the fields and barns in the company of the men of La Cienega.

So she had hidden. Hidden until Milagros found her and dragged her into her own bedroom and forced her to put on one of her older sister's lovely dresses. Then Milagros had wrapped her shaved head with a beautiful blue silk scarf, pinning it up, turban-like, with silver clasps. Ruperto had never seen her without her hat. She had made certain of that. Finished, Milagros and Juanita and Carla the maids put cascara *– face powder – on her cheeks and colouring on her lips, then handsome pearl earrings and a diamond necklace that had been their mother's.*

As they worked over her, Milagros kept whispering into Isadora's ear, 'Do not let this boy go. You may not get another chance. Take this one and get out of here.'

Finished, Milagros dragged her in front of a long mirror. Isadora was stunned. She felt beautiful and feminine. She had never felt that way before. She never would again. Then the four of them were holding hands and dancing and laughing in a circle.

Aba had kept Ruperto occupied on the veranda, plying him with sweet drinks on the hot summer evening. Her father had retired to his room early, as he did each night.

Milagros shoved Isadora out the door of the hacienda towards where Ruperto sat sipping a drink, watched over by Aba. Then the two women withdrew, leaving Isadora alone with him. While awkward, it was not as difficult as she had dreaded. Ruperto was funny and lively, and they were soon laughing and talking. Ruperto told her stories of the great city of Mexico, of his family, of trips he had taken. And Isadora listened. Listened and felt like a young woman. It was a wonderful feeling.

Then suddenly the Patrón was standing before them in his night-shirt, holding a pistol in one hand and a fencing sabre in the other. Blue veins pulsed at the side of his head and he was weaving in one of his drugged stupors. He said nothing, just pointed the cocked pistol at the chest of Ruperto.

Then Aba and Milagros were there, Aba talking the Patrón down in firm but soothing tones, Milagros standing bravely between their father's pistol and the boy. Then the Patrón raised the sabre as if he might strike Milagros with it and instead poked it over her shoulder and deftly lifted the blue turban of silk from Isadora's head, exposing her bare skull before he turned and walked back into the hacienda.

Two days later a body was found on a lonely road south of Los Angeles. It had been dragged for miles behind a horse. Ruperto Tristán was identified by what was left of his clothes.

'Did my father murder the boy, Ruperto Tristán?'

The old woman shrugged again.

'Dorothy Regal?'

The abuela grasped at the rising smoke, flexing her fingers in the drifting fumes and pulling at the grey wisps. Then she dropped her hands into her lap and sagged back into her chair.

'*Cuidado*,' was all she said. 'Be careful.'

The place felt different in broad daylight – muddy and smelling of garbage, but no longer frightening. Sister Ria

136

was bent over at the waist, slowly retracing her steps down the alley, studying the sticky earth beneath her shoes.

She stopped and looked down the empty lane where the figure had disappeared the night before, her muscles tightening. Had she only imagined it? It didn't seem possible. The human shape had been clearly visible in the lamplight, if only for a second. She waited for Clemente Rojo, who was struggling to balance a heavy tripod and camera over his shoulder, to catch up. She took the tripod from him and put it over her shoulder and they walked down the shade-shrouded alley.

Sister Ria had not found what she was hunting, when she pushed open the door to the small storeroom. Clemente touched her arm and she stopped and he pulled out his little pistol and went in first to check the rooms. Then he was back, motioning her inside.

She looked down nervously at the crib then quickly glanced up at the white plaster wall, and froze. The dark smudge of the moth's body was gone, the wall showing no sign that the creature had ever been smashed against it. She shuddered and crossed herself. 'May God protect us,' she whispered. Frantically, she hunted for the broom. It wasn't there either. Clemente watched her.

'Do you want to leave?' he asked, his voice full of concern, his normally serious face even more serious.

She didn't answer.

He bent in front of her and waved his hand in a friendly way. 'Sister, are you in there?'

'Yes, I'm sorry.'

'Do you want to go back?'

'No,' she mumbled, her heart pumping hard.

'Sister, are you sure you're OK?'

'There was a moth –'

Clemente watched her face.

'I smashed it against that wall. You saw it.' She turned and looked at the man. When he didn't respond, she said again, 'You saw it?'

Clemente shook his head. Then when he saw the fright in her eyes he quickly added: 'But I wasn't looking for a smashed moth on the wall.'

'Well, it was there. I killed it.'

Clemente's eyes searched the plaster.

'I killed it,' she whispered again.

'There,' she said.

Rojo set his large mahogany camera on its tripod in the back room and then squatted down beside her and stared at the jumble of muddy footprints tracked inside from the alley.

'Those are mine,' he said.

'Are you sure?'

He stood and placed his boot into the print: a perfect match.

'This is the print we want,' he continued.

She studied the smaller boot print that Clemente was pointing at and nodded. She continued searching over the jumbled collection of footprints. 'None here,' she whispered.

'Sister?'

'There was no child here.'

'It doesn't look like it.'

This thought, that someone had lured her into this place by mimicking a child's voice, caused the hair on the back of her neck to rise.

Rojo was watching her face and looking concerned again. He patted her arm in a comforting way.

138

'I'm fine, thank you.'

Rojo nodded and placed a ruler alongside the boot-print and brought his camera over and began to work with a series of brass screws until the camera's lens was aiming straight down at the floor. Then he began to fiddle with the black cloth bellows, focusing the instrument.

Sister Ria was squatting by the muddy prints when she heard something move in the boxes behind her. She froze. 'Child?' she cried, standing and whirling around.

But it was not a child. Fernando strolled out slowly from behind a stack of yellowed newspapers dragging a paper bag with the lettering *Antonio's Italian Eatery* printed on the side. He sat down, not appearing overly glad to see her. 'Where have you been?' she asked, as if the old cat might stop and tell her. But he seemed to have more important things to do and stuck his head in the bag.

Needing to sit and think, Sister Ria caught a small red horse-drawn streetcar at the corner of Spring and Sixth, running things over and over in her mind. She watched as the car rolled past the intersections of Faith, Hope and Charity, shaking her head at this American-style rosary.

Fernando was sitting next to her, seemingly lost in deep contemplation of his own. Sister Ria and the old cat got off the streetcar at Figueroa Street and walked west down the tree-lined boulevard of expensive old Mexican homes. She was thinking about the moth, the footprints and her father, who he was or was not, and growing more frustrated with every step.

The elegant home of Don José Vargas was surrounded by a high wall protecting it from intruders and road dust.

A servant led her through a heavy door into a tree- and flower-filled courtyard alive with the sounds of parrots and fountains. It reminded her of early Colonial Mexico and her youth.

They were deep in the garden when Sister Ria saw two peones squatting in a large dirt circle shoving fierce-looking fighting cocks – necks extended, hackles flared – at one another. She had seen the rite hundreds of times, and hated it. Fernando apparently did not feel the same and he trotted over to the men.

'Do not let them fight,' she said. The words were like an echo in her mind, her thoughts fragments of a dark past crowding in on her.

It was a warm spring morning and she was snaking wild cattle down out of the hills with the vaqueros of La Cienega, when they jumped him. They had been looking for him for weeks, had seen his kills on the grassy edges of the plains.

Felipe Bacus had dismounted and was hunting strays in a narrow arroyo when he stumbled onto him. The beast's right foreleg was broken. Even so, he was quick and he caught the screaming Bacus in the dense brush.

Isadora reached them first, lunging her large sorrel gelding, Cibola – the bison – straight into the giant bear. Isadora had always resisted riding the huge horse but her father demanded it whenever she worked cattle. She had always believed that he had simply meant to further humiliate her, forcing her to ride an animal that looked like a gigantic plough horse. But in this frightening moment she knew she had been wrong. Though terrified, the huge horse rammed the roaring bear, driving hard with its hoofs in an effort to roll the enormous brute.

The first charge did not stop the bear's mauling of Bacus, and she backed Cibola up for a second run. Isadora could hear the vaqueros urging their mounts up the narrow arroyo behind her, yelling at her to get away. But she would not. While she detested the role, she had replaced her dead brother as the Patroncito of La Cienega. It was her responsibility. And she would not run from it.

Bacus was screaming when she put her spurs to Cibola. Amazingly quick for his size, he slammed his great bulk into the bear, knocking it momentarily off the man, giving Bacus the chance to scramble for his life. Then the others were around her, shielding her, yelling and throwing their ropes on the roaring beast.

Six riders held the lunging bear tethered between their horses by the long ropes, hauling him slowly across the plain, the animal charging first one way and then another, only to be pulled back by the strangling ropes. They dragged him, half choked to death, to the barricaded bull pen behind the horse barn. The Patrón and the vaqueros stood on the wooden rampart staring down at the emaciated beast. Her father was dressed as a medieval English knight in a gold tunic that came to his knobbly knees, a heavy jousting helmet on his head, a short broadsword hanging at his side.

'He's crippled and starving,' she said.

'He tried to kill Bacus,' the Patrón said from inside the helmet.

'Bacus surprised him.'

She watched the herders driving one of the giant range bulls into a chute that opened into the pen – a heavy planked door blocked the bull's entry into the enclosure. 'Do not let them fight,' she said. The bull had smelled its old adversary and was lunging at the thick oak walls of the narrow passage.

The Patrón looked out at her from inside the helmet for a moment. Then he yelled, 'Open the gate!'

The bull took the bear from the side with a powerful lunge, goring the beast deep in its shoulder and driving him roaring into the wall of the pen. The grizzly was no coward and fought back, but the giant bull was too powerful and the bear too weakened by starvation.

The bloody contest had been raging for some ten minutes now, the men drinking hot beer and toasting the combatants, when the explosion shattered the afternoon air. The bear went down without a twitch. The men turned and stared in silence as Isadora leaned the rifle against the rampart wall, climbed down the ladder and began to walk slowly back to the hacienda.

Then in the stillness, the Patrón began to slowly clap.

She shoved her thoughts back to the garden. 'Did you hear me?' she asked in Spanish. Fernando was sitting by the edge of the circle like a spectator in the front row of a prize fight.

Through a nicely trimmed privet hedge, the voice of Don Vargas interrupted her, 'Adolfo, please do as our good Sister requests.'

Sister Ria peered around the side of the hedge. Perhaps to remind himself of his poor pueblo roots, José Vargas was sitting in an old rocking chair under a roughly constructed Indian jacal of upright cottonwood poles and lighter crossbeams of ash, the whole of the three-sided structure covered with thick grape vines. The old man looked weak – not as she remembered him. He bowed his head towards her and crossed himself with a heavy boned hand; an old guitar and a blanket lay on his thin legs.

'Thank you, Don José.'

'Isadora, anything.'

142

She noted his lack of surprise at her sudden return to the pueblo after eight years' absence and her new life as a nun – as if he already knew both. And she guessed he probably did. Over the years of her childhood, Don José had always amazed her with what he knew – minute strands of detail woven into evidence, intelligence, fascinating facts.

If anyone knew what had happened to Dorothy Regal it would be José Vargas. People hired him for the things he knew – Americans as well as Mexicans. He had represented her father during the trial and lost – but still he might have the answer she needed. 'It is wonderful to see you, Don José. You look well,' she lied.

'Old,' he said, 'but you, Sister of the Virgin, are young and very beautiful.' He waved a hand. 'Come sit and talk with me. Pretty girls rarely do any more.'

Sister Ria laughed and walked over and kissed his cheek. The old man had been her father's attorney all her life and her godfather and she loved him dearly. Twice Don Vargas had served as *alcalde* – mayor – of the Pueblo de Los Angeles. But that had been a long time ago. Now he was Los Angeles' only Mexican attorney. Gaunt, his brown eyes sunk deep in their sockets, but still handsome, soft-voiced and silver-haired, he was a man worn down by time.

'It is wonderful to see you,' she said again, putting a hand warmly to the old man's cheek.

'And you, Isadora,' he said, struggling to his feet and laying the guitar and blanket aside. He grasped both of Sister Ria's hands. She could feel a tremor in his arms. Then he sat back down, as if the effort was too much, still smiling at her. He took in the wimple, the stark white scapular, the shapeless cloth.

143

'I had heard of this,' he said, making a proud sweeping gesture with a thin liver-spotted hand at her robes. 'Most lovely of nuns, Sister Ria – I believe.'

'Yes, right as usual.'

'Sister Ria. Wonderful.'

She glanced at the garden and the house. 'You look as successful as always, Don José.'

'Only modestly able to survive.' The teasing sound left his voice. 'How is the Patrón?'

Sister Ria just nodded.

The old man studied her face and started to say something and then seemed to change his mind and let her little act of rudeness pass unchallenged.

They sat in the shade of the jacal and laughed and chatted about times past, and she relaxed for the first time since she had come back. Listening to Don Vargas' voice, she remembered why she had always loved him: *He had been what her father had not: interested in her and caring.* The servants brought steaming cups of dark coffee and small rich sugar cakes. Sister Ria balanced the cup and a cloth napkin on her thigh for a while before she set it on a side table and looked at the old man, her expression suddenly serious.

'The men at the Gas Company –'

'How is Milagros?'

'Fine. She'll see the American Governor, asking for a postponement of the execution.' She paused and studied the old man's face. 'Will he grant it?'

Vargas shrugged. 'It is hard to say. He refused when I asked him several weeks ago. But Milagros can be very convincing.'

'Do you believe what she believes?'

'About Summerville and Atkins?'

'Yes.'

'I had men I trust look into it. They found nothing. It is true they tried to buy La Brea. They made offers, through me, many times. But that doesn't make them murderers.' The old man took a sip of coffee, his hand dwarfing the small cup, then he set it on the table and sat watching the steam rising from the dark liquid.

She massaged her forehead with the tips of her fingers.

'Why have you come back, Sister Ria?' he asked.

'I promised my mother the day she died that I would take care of him.' She paused. 'It was a childish promise.'

'You are grown now. You have a life with God.'

She nodded. 'Yes.' They sat without speaking for a time. 'But I still have the promise.'

Don José gazed across the garden at a pair of red and green Mexican parrots sitting on a perch near the stone fountain. 'As a young man your father dreamed of being a great artist. He studied in France and Italy and was considered very promising in that world. So promising that he had been taken on as a student by Frederico de Madrazo, one of Spain's greatest artists. We had grown up together, were as close as brothers, and I knew how thrilled he was by the chance to work under such a great painter. But it was not to be.'

She looked at him but said nothing.

'Your grandfather Raúl Simón was dying, and Maximiato was told that he must return and take over the affairs of La Cienega and the Lugo family.' Don José pursed his lips and continued to study the parrots. 'And he did so. He gave up his dream. Just like like smoke in the wind – it disappeared. He became the Patrón of La Cienega.'

Sister Ria stared at the ground in front of her.

145

'Your brother Ramón was being trained to take your father's place in the long line of Lugo men who have taken care of the fortunes of the Lugo family. It is the Spanish way, Sister Ria,' he said, knowing full well she knew. He paused. 'Then Ramón died.'

'And I replaced him,' she whispered.

'Yes. There was no one else.'

'Milagros.'

Don José smiled and shook his head. 'Milagros would not have done it. She could not have been relied upon. Your father knew that – he knew he could place his trust and the future of the Lugo family in your hands.'

'He had no right.'

'Perhaps. Or perhaps he had the right of a thousand years of the Spanish way of life.'

She rubbed her face in her hands and then looked at Don José and said, 'He has lost his mind.'

The old man's eyes met hers. He didn't speak for a time. Finally, he said, 'He has aged. We all have aged. Minds change.' He gazed out at his garden as if he had finished, then took a deep breath. 'But not hearts.'

José Vargas appeared to have gone to sleep in the sunlight. Finally, he stirred and looked at her. 'Don Maximiato did not kill that woman. But I cannot prove it.' He drifted off again. Then a male servant in white came and touched him on his arm. 'Don José – it is past your rest time.'

Sister Ria's hopes fell. She had believed that Don José would help her reason through what little she had in the way of information. But he could not. He was too old, too feeble.

'He was my friend and I let him down,' Vargas mumbled.

'You did all you could. I know you.'

146

He sat up straighter, holding onto the servant's hand, and looked at Sister Ria. 'Don Lugo should have taken it.'

'Taken what, Don José?'

'Their offer. It was generous; the few acres they wanted are worthless. He has little left.'

She looked surprised. 'He has 37,000 acres.'

'Most is gone.' Don José picked up his cup and drained the last of the coffee, the hand shaking, and handed it to the servant. 'The American taxes.' He paused a moment. 'The seventies' drought destroyed most of the cattle and sheep, leaving the patróns no way to pay.'

The sun was no longer on Vargas' face and he scooted his chair to catch it, the way she had seen lizards move to the sunlight to drive the chill out of their bodies.

The servant stood patiently by, gently resting a hand on the old man's shoulder. 'Then the Anglo squatters came and challenged the legitimacy of the title grants and the ranchos were forced to prove ownership.' He shook his head, blue veins pulsing at his temples. 'It is an impossible task – the land grants are a hundred years old, vague boundaries. Your father had me fight them for years. I hired Anglo lawyers who knew the American laws. All of that cost money –'

'How much is left?'

'Of La Cienega?'

'Yes.'

'Perhaps 1,000 arpents. No more.'

She drew in a sharp breath. Thirty-six thousand acres – Lugo family land for almost a hundred years – gone to pay taxes. It did not seem possible.

The old man's eyes were shut again, his face turned up to the sun. She waited for him to look at her. When he

147

did not, she said, 'I found a book of Tennyson in her room.'

'The Patrón did not kill the woman, Isadora.'

'And a piece of paper with the words *curandera* and *brown cutaway* written on them. Did any of these things come up during the trial?'

He shook his head no.

'Do you know what they might mean?'

'I know only that the Patrón is not a murderer.'

'Can you be sure?'

'I know the Patron,' Vargas said, patting the servant's hand indicating he would like to get to his feet. He looked at Sister Ria. 'I am old now, you must excuse me. It is good for these eyes of mine to see your lovely face.' He stopped talking and gazed at her. 'Do you remember what I used to call you?'

She nodded. '*La niña testaruda.*'

He smiled, 'Sí, the stubborn child.' He paused. 'You should not be stubborn any longer.' He watched her face for a time before he said, 'Forgive him – for your own sake.'

She said nothing.

'You should be proud of him, as I am proud to call him my friend.'

She shook her head and said, 'He is not worth being proud of.'

Don José settled back into the chair as if her refusal had further weakened him. 'He is a great man.' He tipped his head up and gazed through the vines overhead at the blue sky above, seemingly searching through his memories. 'When we were young we went out with General Pico to fight the Yankees the day they came for our land. We met them in Cahuenga Pass. There were hundreds of them

148

and only sixty or seventy of us.' Don Vargas began to chuckle. 'And General Pico determined in all his soldiering wisdom that a hasty retreat was strategically wise for our cause.' The old man smirked. 'I agreed wholeheartedly.' He paused and caught his breath. 'But not your father.'

Don Vargas pulled himself up straighter in the chair, his face turning sombre. 'He flew into one of his furies – ranting and raging, exhorting us to battle. But we were not convinced, and after a frustrating time spent challenging us to do our duty, he marched off to his tent.' The old man looked at her. 'We all thought he was done. But you know him, Isadora.'

She pursed her lips and nodded. It was not the most flattering of looks but it matched her feelings.

'Minutes later Don Maximiato came clanging back, dressed in the ancient battle armour of a proud lancer of the conquistadores, yelling "Who will join me in ridding our land of these *perros*?"' Don José was chuckling softly again. 'I will say that he looked very impressive. But I am ashamed to add that none of us agreed to join him in ridding the land of the Yankee dogs. Instead we tried to reason with him – which, as you know, Isadora, is a task equal to talking the moon out of the night sky.

'When Maxie finally became convinced that we were all cowards and would never join him, he screamed, "Hoist me onto my horse!"' The look on the old man's face had turned grave.

'Don José,' she whispered, 'you need to rest.'

He shook his head as if a wasp had buzzed his ear.

'None of us would do it. Not until he looked at me and said, "José, you must." I remember to this day the look in his eyes. It made me proud to be his friend.' Don José wiped his mouth with his napkin. '"You will be

149

killed," I told him. "Yes," he said, "but our honour will live."' Don José dabbed at his eyes, suddenly overcome with emotion. 'And so I helped him onto his horse.'

'I was frightened and ashamed, and your father saw that and he looked at me and said, "It is all right, José. I fight this day for us both because even though I know you would, you must not. You must care for my wife and guide my son in protecting the Lugo family." Then he spurred his horse up and down in front of us yelling, "You have one last chance to join me!" When no one stepped forward, he trotted his little horse out across the plain, his lance under his arm, calling in a loud voice, "For the King of Spain and honour!"'

The old man stopped talking and gazed down at the ground as if he could still see Don Maximiato trotting forward between the two opposing armies. 'None of us thought he would actually do it – that he was simply full of foolish bravado and would soon whirl his mount and return to us, satisfied he had faced the enemy. But he did not. One moment he had stopped and was sitting silently on his grand little stallion – small like David facing Goliath – then the next, he was spurring his mount across the wide space, leaning forward with almost perfect lancer form.' The old man was breathing hard, sweat breaking on his brow. 'The Americans were laughing at him, they too expected him to turn and flee back to us. We stood dumbstruck by his courage. And then they began to fire.

'We could hear the bullets striking his armour. His horse staggered and almost went down from the withering fire but Don Lugo spurred it to its feet and together they continued their charge. The Americans were no longer laughing.'

'He survived,' she said, as if determined to strip him of any glory.

Don José nodded. 'Yes, he survived. How, I do not know.'

The old man was shaking his head, gazing into the back-eddies of his mind. 'We were certain he was dead and, fearing that his bold act of bravery would trigger a charge from the Americans, we turned and were quickly leaving the field, sadly defeated without firing a shot, when suddenly a cheer went up and we turned back and saw the Patrón break free of the American lines and gallop back out onto the plain and stop. He and his little horse – both of them gravely wounded – were about to collapse. Everyone on both sides just stood and stared in silent, almost reverent disbelief at this small, brave man, who had become a giant to us on the Mexican side.'

Don José turned his head and looked at Sister Ria. 'None of us said anything. I could not look at my friend. His courage had shamed me. Then I heard a man next to me whisper, "Madre de Dios," and I looked up to see the Patrón spurring his little wounded stallion back into the American lines. We watched them both go down.'

'He survived,' she said again.

'With God's grace. He had been shot seven times – but he survived.'

Sister Ria helped the servant lift Don Vargas from his chair. The old man stood watching her for a moment, worn down by the telling of the story, then he said, 'Forgive him before his death.' He patted the servant's arm and they turned and started towards the rear of the house.

'Don José,' she said, watching Vargas and the servant. 'I love you,' she called.

They stopped and the old man stood looking at her, and then he smiled and waved. The servant began to lead him down the path again. Sister Ria was standing and watching them and straightening her habit when she felt it: the piece of paper that Milagros had given her.

She had nowhere else to go.

THIRTEEN

The gas company offices were located on the north-east corner of Second and Spring streets in a tall, imposing building of Texas red stone, with demonic gargoyles and griffons perched on each high corner. She crossed herself at the sight of them, fighting the confusion in her mind and rubbing her eyes with the tips of her fingers, exhausted and focusing on the glass door of the building. Fearing that if she hesitated she might never do it, she forced herself to push through the swinging doors.

'Mr Summerville will see you now.'

Sister Ria followed the young American secretary whose brass name plate identified her as Marjorie Sullivan into a room that looked like a parlour with rich leather sofas and chairs, the walls panelled with dark oak and handsomely appointed with heavy brass fixtures and paintings of lush green English hunt scenes that seemed out of place in this desert land. Was this the office of Dorothy Regal's murderer, as Milagros believed?

'Please be seated,' Miss Sullivan smiled. The girl,

seventeen or eighteen at the most, Sister Ria thought, was grinning and bouncy and chewing on the end of a pencil and eyeing Sister Ria like she had never seen a Sister of the cloth in the flesh before.

'What's it like?' she whispered.

'I'm not sure what you mean.'

'What it's like to be a nun? Don't you miss things?'

'We have things to occupy us.'

'Praying? Do you pray all day? I've heard that. That sounds so boring.'

Sister Ria focused on the girl – she was sweet and kid-like innocent and Sister Ria smiled. 'The contemplative orders pray much of the time. We don't pray all day in my order, the Benedictines.'

The girl chewed on the pencil a little more and then asked, 'So what do you do?'

Sister Ria smiled again and said, 'I work with dying lepers.'

The expression on Miss Sullivan's face transformed instantly, as if she had seen her own death mask. She began backing towards the door. 'Please – please be seated,' she said.

'Thank you,' Sister Ria called but Miss Sullivan was gone. She sat in a chair in front of an elegant old burl desk of exceptional beauty, with lovely gold-plated handles and claw-footed feet, polished to a glistening sheen.

Having nothing better to do, Fernando sat on the floor next to her, looking bored. Sister Ria waited a few seconds and then stood and hurriedly searched through the shelves behind the desk for the book of Tennyson. Not there. Quickly, she pulled open each drawer of the desk and peeked inside. Not there either. Suddenly ashamed of herself for prying through another's belongings like a common thief, she sat back down in the chair and anxiously awaited the man's arrival.

Ten minutes later the office door opened.

Sister Ria's head was inclined slightly, her hands clasped tightly, her lips moving in a one-sided talk with the archangel Gabriel, when Summerville walked into the room. She was not certain what she expected the man to look like – but she expected him to look different than he did. He was small, with bright red hair, a wiry build and a priestly smile. She liked him immediately.

'Good afternoon,' he said, cheerfully looking at Sister Ria. 'I have been warned that you have leprosy.' He laughed. 'I would say you are holding up quite well.'

'I work in a hospital for lepers – I don't have the disease.'

He looked serious for a moment. 'It must be very sad work.'

She nodded. 'At times, very sad.'

The man looked down at Fernando and his face brightened. 'I thought witches had cats for companions – not nuns.' He laughed again. She could hear the harsh sounds of a brass band starting up in the street outside. Summerville walked to the window.

'We aren't companions,' she said. 'He just follows me.'

'Really.' He grinned. 'You look to be the best of friends.' He was looking down at the street and shaking his head at something.

Fernando sat licking a cowlick on his stomach. He did not seem to like the man as much as she did, and he kept his one eye locked on him. When the old cat had grown tired of licking hair, he made his move, leaping up onto Summerville's beautiful burl desk.

Sister Ria snapped her fingers at the cat. Fernando ignored her and sniffed a few expensive-looking silver

155

items, nosed roughly through some papers and almost tipped over a half-full cup of coffee. Summerville glanced at him but didn't seem bothered by the old cat strolling around over his beautiful desk.

'Fernando,' she said.

'He's fine,' the man said. 'Let him enjoy himself. He looks as if he's had a tough life.' Summerville turned back to the window, his interest perking at something beyond the glass. 'Your family has lived here, what, forty years?'

'Closer to one hundred,' she said.

'Then you'll definitely find this interesting, Sister,' he continued, nodding towards the glass.

She walked over.

The parade was headed down Second Street towards the railroad terminal. Two riders wearing red sombreros sat astride a pair of matched chestnut geldings at the head of a column of marching bands and festive floats, stretching a canvas sign between them that read: *First Train of California Oranges Shipped to New York*. The street was crowded with people.

'Outstanding – an entire train filled with our oranges shipped all the way to Eastern markets. Los Angeles is growing up, Sister,' he said, proudly. Sister Ria stood watching the parade while Summerville walked behind his desk and sat in a green velvet swivel chair. He picked up a thin black cigar, paying absolutely no attention to the huge cat sleeping on his ink blotter. Sister Ria liked the man for that.

'Do you mind?' he asked, holding up the cigar.

'Not at all.'

'Thank you,' he said, striking a match and smiling at her again. The sun was warm on the old feline and Fernando was purring loudly, as if to try and goad the man.

It wasn't working.

'It is good to finally meet you,' Summerville said, his voice sincere.

'Don José Vargas doesn't think you would murder.' She watched his face for a reaction.

He smiled. 'You don't waste a lot of time warming up to things.'

'I don't have any time.'

'I understand,' he said, his voice sympathetic. 'We didn't frame your father like your sister believes.'

'Or murder Dorothy Regal?'

'Of course not,' he said quickly, his voice rising slightly. 'Do you know what it's like, Sister, to have people saying things about you, whispering behind your back?'

She did, but she said nothing.

'I have small children, for God's sake.' He quickly held up his hands, as if surrendering. 'I'm sorry. Forgive me.'

She nodded.

'Our crime, Sister, was trying to buy a few acres,' he said, licking his lips. 'Edison Electric has crashed the price of street lighting in America. We can't continue to ship coal from Australia. Not and stay in business.' He stopped and studied her across his desk.

She didn't say anything.

'We offered far more for your father's land than it could possibly be worth.'

She stiffened. 'And what is my family's heritage worth on the American market?'

He made a steeple of his fingers, looking over them at her, seemingly reappraising her, as if he had not expected anything but kindness and prayers from a Sister of the veil. Then he turned his head and yelled, 'Sam!'

The side door opened and a thin bespectacled man with

a fringe of greyish hair like a long-dead Christmas wreath stepped through the door. 'Luke?'

This man looked less dangerous than Summerville.

'Sam, this is Sister Ria, the younger daughter of Max Lugo.'

Sister Ria did not care for this Anglicized version of her father's name. 'Don Maximiato Rialto Lugo, El Patrón of La Cienega,' she said stiffly.

'Yes, I'm sorry,' he said, looking, she thought, more annoyed than apologetic. 'Don Lugo.' He glanced at his partner. 'What was the amount we offered for the acreage?'

'Seventy-five,' Sam Atkins said, his voice high pitched, almost childlike.

'Seventy-five thousand, Sister. For seventy-five thousand dollars I can buy a 3,000 acre ranch. Now that's a fair price for five acres of land, isn't it?'

She raised herself up slowly from the chair, her eyes fixed on Samuel Atkins.

'Is everything all right, Sister?' Summerville asked, his voice less friendly than before.

Atkins watched her like she might be daft.

She didn't care. The man's voice had sounded childlike and she could not stop thinking of the small voice calling to her from the darkness of the alley . . . and Milagros' certain belief that these men had framed her father for the killing of Dorothy Regal.

'Are you all right?' Summerville asked again.

She stared at the two men. 'Do either of you read poetry?' It was a goad rather than a question.

'Not really,' Summerville said.

Atkins shook his head no.

'Then you wouldn't have a leather-bound book of poems by Tennyson?'

Summerville watched her for a moment and then said, 'No. Is that what you were going through my desk for?'

His voice was no longer friendly. The muscles of her back tightened. He had been watching her somehow as she rifled his office. The thought frightened her.

'Yes,' she said and walked out.

Sister Ria was moving slowly, etherized by her worries. Summerville and Atkins did not look like murderers. She shook her head, knowing that she had no idea what a murderer looked like. The man Samuel Atkins – with his high voice – could have been the person calling to her from the alley.

She wandered aimlessly up and down the busy street in front of the Gas Company searching her mind for what to do next. The parade was gone but not the crowds. It was almost dark. Brown bats were stitching through the night sky hunting insects in the light of the gas lamps. There was a festive mood on the streets, vendors hawking goods, mariachis playing lively tunes, people strolling, children darting in and out of the crowd and setting off strings of Mexican *buscapies* – firecrackers, the stores open.

An hour later she was still pacing the sidewalk, when she suddenly felt uneasy and looked up and caught a glimpse of the small man in the brown suit and black fedora on the opposite side of the street. He was sliding through the crowd, watching her. Then he realized she had seen him and he ducked away, turning quickly into a nearby building.

She'd had enough.

She dodged through the road traffic and entered the building the man had disappeared into, just as he was leaving through the back door. The structure housed a

159

large dry goods emporium packed with shoppers. She hurried after the little man, weaving and bumping her way through the aisles jammed with people.

Sister Ria was moving fast as she went out the back door into the deepening shadows of night pooling on a narrow roadway. The little man was some fifty yards ahead of her, just disappearing around a corner. He was carrying a satchel of some kind. She trotted after him. When she rounded the same corner, she expected to see him walking down the road. He was not. He was also trotting. He looked back, saw her, and ducked quickly down a side road. Sister Ria pulled the hem of her habit up to her knees and started to run. She had had it with this man's games.

The narrow road was lined on both sides with heavy adobe walls. She stopped. The little man was standing at the far end, holding the satchel in both hands. Sister Ria squinted, trying to make out the man's features, but the distance and the shadows were too great for her to see the man's face.

He started off again.

The night was deepening and she was barely able to see the figure. Again, she settled down to running. Who was she chasing? From his size and shape, it could be her father – or Samuel Atkins. Whoever it was, he was involved in the murder of Dorothy Regal. She was certain of it.

They were on the outskirts of town now, trotting down a small dirt road through empty fields. One moment, she was glimpsing the man running ahead of her in the growing darkness. The next, he was gone. She stopped and stood in the middle of the road, alert for movement, trying to see the figure in the failing light. When she could not, she edged into the bushes at the side of the road and waited.

Had he doubled back on her? Was he at this very moment sneaking through the darkness towards her? She started to tremble, then pulled herself up to her full height. She would not be cowed by evil.

The dusty road was on the northern edge of town and edged with pepper and cottonwood trees, empty of houses and people. It was used during the day by the poor Mexicans who followed it to the river to collect their daily water. No one would be collecting water at night. She was certain the little man knew this. She listened but heard no sounds that seemed out of place – only dogs barking and the wind and the voice of a street vendor somewhere in the far distance.

Was she being watched, she wondered? What did he want? Was it Atkins? He would have had time to change his clothes after she had walked out of Summerville's office.

She started to move forward, then stopped. He might be anywhere ahead of her. Her mind leaped to Milagros' warning. He might be waiting to kill her. Long minutes passed. She studied the ebony landscape. She saw nothing but a wall of blackness where the trees were. She heard no sound, saw nothing but the empty road and the dark sky above. Growing tense and agitated with the waiting, she slowly retraced her steps back up the dusty lane, back toward town, bent over and walking to the side of the road, searching until she found the small boot prints in the dirt. From the size and shape, they could have been her father's.

She crept forward again in the darkness. He might be stalking her – but now she was stalking him as well. The thought made her feel better. She followed the prints until they turned off the roadway and up a narrow sandy path through the brush, into a stand of cottonwood trees. No sound except the pounding of the blood in her temples. Then she heard a small animal-like squeal in the darkness. She crouched down and listened.

Nothing more.

The moon was rising, its pallid light barely illuminating the trees. She stood and bent over again, peering at the earth, when the moon disappeared behind clouds and the thicket was suddenly awash in deeper darkness. She waited a moment and gathered herself. She could see little beneath the thick canopy of leaves – but Sister Ria had spent her youth tracking coyotes and mountain lions in this land. She was no amateur at the hunt. And she moved slowly forward, on blind instinct.

Then suddenly she stopped. Something was ahead of her.

Leaves stirred. She jumped. Nothing else. No movement. No sound other than the wind in the trees. Sister Ria was beginning to question the sensation pulsing in her head that she was not alone, when she saw it.

It was small and childlike, hanging in the darkness at the end of a cord tied to a tree branch. She inched forward, fighting the panic growing in her. Then as she got closer her eyes made it out in the shadows and she screamed and ran and grasped the tiny shape. But it was not what she thought and she let go of it and backed away, her hands covered in blood. The figure swung slowly back and forth in the night air, kicking out the last of its life. Then it went limp, its struggle over. It was a small cur dog, its throat cut – its body shrouded in a roughly sewn black robe, a nun's habit. Then the moonlight pierced a gap in the trees and she saw a spark of red at the dog's throat. Trembling, she stepped forward until she could make out the object in the blackness. She clamped down on the air moving in and out of her windpipe: the garnet brooch – the one taken from her room.

In an angry rush beyond reason or fear, she yanked the jewellery from the poor lifeless animal and began to back away down the path. The man in the brown suit had just sent her a cruel warning: *He had been inside the hacienda. Inside her bedroom. And she would die if she persisted in her search.*

The realization was numbing.

'You will not scare me!' she shouted.

'I'm not afraid of you!' Her voice seemed to freeze all sound around her in the night. Birds no longer stirred in the trees, there was no insect noise; even the wind had stopped. She began backing towards the road.

She was about to move into the lane, when suddenly she heard something rushing towards her. She squealed and whirled to see Fernando trotting through the darkness, the old cat grumbling about something.

'Shhhh,' she hissed, searching the darkened road with her eyes again. Still empty.

But the old feline would not be quiet. His hair standing up, gnashing his teeth and spitting at an invisible foe, he stalked back and forth in front of her. He had been acting like her personal guardian from that first night at the hacienda. She was about to tell him to be quiet when he stopped moving and stood gazing off into the darkness.

'What?' she asked, her voice low. The cat ignored her, his eye glued on the carbon blackness. She looked past him: the path was still empty as far as she could tell, but the look of the old tom said something quite different. She shoved the brooch into her pocket so her hands were free and stood sucking in small bites of air, trying to decide what to do.

163

Then she felt movement somewhere ahead of her and she peered again into the darkness, and shuddered. She could see the orange ash of a cigarette. The man was standing in the centre of the lane, watching her, waiting for her. As soon as Fernando saw the shadowy shape he started towards it, shrieking like some sort of enraged primal beast defending against the night leopard. Sister Ria ran and grabbed him up in her arms. The old cat was hissing madly.

'I am not afraid of you!' she shouted again.

The figure did not move.

Then the ash flared again like a warning beacon in a dark sea and Sister Ria turned, Fernando locked in her arms, and trotted back towards town, the cat looking over her shoulder and clicking his teeth and hissing. She leaned her head into him and he hissed louder.

The second deeply unsettling occurrence of the night came minutes later, as she stood in the middle of the still crowded sidewalk on Main Street with people grumbling and pushing around her. She didn't care – she just stood gaping open-mouthed at the large red banner hanging above the emporium's front door. She had put Fernando down moments before and the old cat had disappeared into the crowd. Sister Ria read the words slowly, then darted into the store and grabbed a salesgirl and dragged her outside and pointed up at the sign like she had just spotted a gorilla on the roof. 'What is that?'

The girl looked frightened. 'Pardon?'

'Tell me what that means?'

The girl studied Sister Ria's face and then the sign, as if she did not understand.

'Tell me!'

The woman tracked Sister Ria's eyes to the banner again:
MEN'S CUTAWAYS – ON SALE THIS MONTH.

'A sale – we're having a sale,' the girl stammered.

'No, not that. What is a cutaway?'

The girl appeared frightened by the look on Sister Ria's
face. 'It's a man's suit, no tails – just a jacket – cut away
here,' she said, pointing at a spot a few inches below her
hip. Sister Ria let go of the girl's arm, her own arms dropping to her side, her eyes still gazing up at the banner.
Then without saying anything more she walked slowly
down the crowded street, the salesgirl watching her as if
she were deranged.

She sat down on a bench and read the words pencilled
at the bottom of the little piece of paper: *Brown cutaway.*
Her throat was tightening, as if someone was choking her.
The figure in the brown suit had been following Dorothy
Regal.

Now he was following her.

FOURTEEN

The ride from town seemed endlessly long and Sister Ria was trying to calm herself, anxious at being confined to a carriage seat while her mind went running off in a hundred different directions. But at least it forced her to face the frightening fact that the man in the brown suit had been in her bedroom . . . that the hacienda was not safe. Millie was right. But she was right as well: their father had gone mad. She was certain he was the man in the brown suit.

Suddenly a flock of sparrows roosting in a hedge of wild rose on the side of the road exploded into the night sky. She whirled on the carriage seat and stared into the darkness. 'You leave me alone!' Sister Ria shouted, startling the little carriage horse into a gallop.

She let him run.

Some fifteen minutes later the animal came to a stop in front of La Cienega's grand barn and Sister Ria crawled down, ashamed that she, a maidservant of the Lord, had given in to the fear of evil. 'I will not be afraid,' she whispered. 'I will not,' she told herself, and walked into the barn. 'Auel?' she called, peeking through the open door of the old stablemaster's sitting room at the familiar posters of famous Mexican fighting bulls and European race-horses. A lantern was burning but the old man was not there. The room was neat as always, but there was a sense of abandonment about it. Remembering the shadow of the night before, she ran her eyes nervously over the dark cavernous insides of the building. Then she shook her head – how quickly she abandoned her faith. Angry at her weaknesses, she marched off into the barn.

'Auel?' she called again.

She dropped the horse's reins to the ground, the little animal stopping and standing obediently while she walked on and turned up the wicks in the kerosene wall sconces, light swelling inside the enormous room. She continued walking, turning in a slow circle and gazing at the gigantic stone structure. The building was 600 feet long and contained exercise rings, equipment and feed rooms, a veterinarian's dispensary, grooming areas and stalls for some sixty horses. She counted only four animals this night, and the building was dirty and badly in need of repairs. Pigeons were nesting in the high rafters, their heads bobbing nervously as they watched her moving below, their filthy droppings coating everything.

When she was a child the Patrón had kept a young Bedouin falconer and his desert hawks moving through the barns and sheds of the rancho, ready to toss the fierce birds into the air at any pigeon foolish enough to enter a La Cienega building. Those times were gone.

She began to shake: six days and he would be dead. How many times had she wished that very thing? God forgive me. How many awful times?

Auel came running into the barn, sliding to a stop in

front of Sister Ria. The little man was breathing hard and yanked his straw hat from his head. 'I am sorry, Señora Lugo,' he mumbled, taking the reins of the little carriage horse.

'There's nothing to be sorry about, Auel.'

She watched as the man hurriedly unhitched the horse from the buggy.

'The Patrón is called Santo, Auel.'

'Yes, he is truly sainted – he has given us a church.'

'The old plaza church, Nuestra Señora, is it not yours?'

The old man shook his head. 'It belongs to the Anglos. They pay American dollars for seats, Señora. We cannot. And the priests are Francos or Italianos.'

'But it is still your church.'

He shook his head again. 'The mass is spoken in inglés –'

'It is still your church,' she insisted.

'They do not want us there. We are nothing to them.' He smiled up at her. 'But the Patrón – he provides for us. He made bigger the Lugo chapel and he marries us, and baptizes our young, buries our dead.'

'He is not a priest,' she said softly.

'No, he is a saint. That is far better than a mere padre.'

She turned and picked up the large envelope lying on the carriage seat. It contained the photograph of the boot print that Clemente Rojo had given her that afternoon. 'Thank you, Auel.' She would not debate God's will and canon law with the old man.

Night was thickening inside the great house. Sister Ria was standing in her father's room catching her breath and holding Clemente Rojo's photograph and feeling terribly anxious, as if she were on the verge of some dark breakup of her soul.

168

She was about to lose her father. And no matter what she thought about him, it was a frightening reality that caused her to hurt somewhere deep inside. Her thoughts were jumbled and she had to struggle to stay focused on anything more than a moment. She who had dedicated her entire being to a spiritual life was now being undone by her human nature and frailties.

Mother, help me, she whispered.

Trembling, she laid the large photograph on the floor in front of the large French armoire and opened the beautiful walnut doors. Then she removed one of the Patrón's tall riding boots, the same boots he had been wearing under his religious vestments in the chapel the night before.

Estrella was standing behind her, dressed in a bone-white servant's dress, a laced shoe on one foot and a sock on her other, her hair pulled up into a neat bun high on her head. Aba had done what she had asked.

'Would you have me polish the Patrón's boots?' Estrella asked.

'No, Estrella. You must go. Aba would not want you in my father's room.'

The girl curtseyed and walked to the door and stopped. 'Thank you, Blessed Sister,' she said. 'For everything. You are as blessed as the Patrón.'

'I am not blessed, Estrella. Neither is the Patrón.'

'Sí, you are both blessed,' the girl insisted.

'It is God who is blessed,' she said. 'Now go.'

Sister Ria sank to her knees beside the picture, holding the boot in her hands, then placed the sole down on top of the photograph. With the edges of the muddy print in the photo blurred, it was not a perfect match. Close but not perfect. She tried another boot with the same result: she wasn't certain. Still, it was close. And it was the only thing that made sense. He was the only person who knew the gardens and the house well enough to have stolen into her room in broad daylight and taken the brooch and scarf without being stopped by the servants. And for the same reason, he was the only one who could have killed the rooster in her room and then slipped back into the house – and Cristina had seen him with the crib.

It had to be him.

Sister Ria searched the closet for the brown cutaway jacket. Nothing. She sat down hard in a nearby chair. Estrella watched her from the open doorway, a look of concern growing on her young face. Unable to restrain herself, Estrella poured a glass of water and took it to Sister Ria, who drank it down.

'Thank you, Estrella, but you must leave. You must not be found in this room.' Sister Ria looked into the girl's face. 'You must be careful in this house.' The young girl helped her up from her chair.

'I don't understand, Blessed Sister.'

'You must always lock the doors – both the hall and garden doors – to my room when you sleep. Do you hear? And you must go nowhere alone with the Patrón. Nowhere. That is a rule you must never forget. Do you understand?'

The girl looked frightened.

'Tell me that you understand, child,' Sister Ria said, grasping Estrella's hands.

The girl nodded, her eyes wide.

There was still the faint smell of her mother's perfumes and bath powders drifting in the air of the closet amongst her mother's clothing. Kneeling on the floor and crying hard, Sister Ria clutched in desperation at a dress hanging

170

in front of her. 'There is nothing I can do for him. Nothing!' Her voice turned into a moan.

She stood up slowly.

'I can't save him.' She buried her face in the cloth.

Some three hours later Sister Ria was sitting in the library working at the long table under the light of a single candle, trying to chart all that had happened over the past few days – all that she knew about Dorothy Regal's murder. She stopped writing and studied the page. She had little more than a jumble of confusing fragments of facts and theories and suspicions. Sister Ria shook her head and started writing again, then stopped and listened. Someone was crying; the noise was faint but she could hear it. She got up and walked into the hallway, turning towards the kitchen. The sound was coming from that direction and growing louder. She hurried down the hallway towards it. As she was approaching the room, she heard Aba's voice. The old woman sounded angry.

'Aba?' Sister Ria said, walking into the darkened kitchen. It was empty but the back door was open and she could see the glow of lanterns burning in the small square where the large earthen ovens were located, and she stepped outside.

Aba was standing with her arms crossed over her thin breasts. The young maid, Cristina, was in front of the old servant holding a large butcher knife and looking frightened.

'I can't do it!' Cristina moaned.

'You will do it.'

'Aba?' Sister Ria asked.

The old woman neither turned nor answered her. But Cristina turned towards Sister Ria and moaned, 'I can't do it – please don't make me, Señora!'

'Cristina,' Aba snapped, 'I have told you before that you are not to bother the Doña. I will not tell you again.'

'Aba?'

'I am simply doing my job, Señora, directing the servants.'

'I am sure you are. And what are you directing Cristina to do?'

The woman did not answer but Sister Ria could see that her body had stiffened at the interference. She was not used to having her directions to the servants questioned.

'Aba?'

'Give me the knife,' Aba said sternly to the sobbing girl. 'Give it to me now.'

The old woman took the knife and walked over to the far wall of the enclosure. Sister Ria squinted into the shadows. They were hanging by their feet – four large brown hens – tied to the wall with cords. Aba grabbed the head of the first bird and pulled its neck out until Sister Ria thought the head must surely pop off, the bird's body going stiff, its wings spreading out. Then, with a quick slice of the knife blade, she decapitated the hen, the bird falling back against the wall, wings flapping hard, blood spurting. Aba stepped quickly away to the second bird.

'I have directed Cristina to prepare the birds for tomorrow's meals,' she snapped, cutting the head off the second bird with the same efficient slice of the knife. 'It is to be part of her job in the future.'

The girl had turned away from the slaughter and looked ready to faint.

The four hens were beating out the last of their lives against the wall when Sister Ria said, 'I am sure there is

172

other work that is more suitable for Cristina, Aba.' She could not take her eyes off the dying hens and the blood sprays, recalling the rooster that had been killed in her bedroom. 'I am certain there is other work for Cristina,' she repeated.

Aba did not turn to face Sister Ria. 'It is the job of the head servant to assign work, Señora.'

'I understand. And I am sure you agree that Cristina is not suited for this work. Please find something else for her to do, Aba.'

The old woman did not respond.

'Aba?'

The woman tipped her head stiffly. 'As you direct, Señora.'

'Thank you,' Sister Ria said, turning to look at the young servant, who was sobbing without sound. 'Cristina, please go to your quarters. Aba will have something for you in the morning.'

Sister Ria waited until Cristina was gone. Then she looked at the old woman, who still stood with her back to her. 'Aba, I want Cristina assigned to normal house chores. Do you understand? She is not to be punished for having spoken to me.'

Aba said nothing.

Sister Ria walked back inside.

Later that same night the clicking of the metal-capped heels of Sister Ria's heavy convent shoes on the loggia tiles reverberated like castanets through the silence of the great hallway. The rooms were quiet, the servants off for the night. She walked slowly towards the only other sound: the faint chanting of a Buddhist mantra in the central courtyard.

Sister Ria stepped out into the garden. The chanting had stopped. Oriental prayer chimes gave off a soft shimmering sound in the warm night air. She saw him through a screen of ivy: painting at his easel, under the light of two lanterns hung on iron tripods, dressed in the brown cloak of a monk, the cowl up over his head, his waist girded with a rough hemp rope.

'Father?' She could see his brush-strokes rapidly creating a rose in the shadowy light, the strokes almost furious. The painted blossom looked a living thing and her mind jumped to thoughts of her sister Milagros and their childhood game. 'Pray for her soul,' she whispered. Sister Ria moved closer, her eyes focused on the cowl. The material blurred before her eyes, worry and lack of sleep overwhelming her. She forced herself to concentrate.

'How are you, Father?'

'Do you know that you will find Pythagoras' Theory of Divisions in the work of all the great masters? Botticelli, Rembrandt, Vermeer –'

'I don't want to talk about that. I want to talk about you.'

'No.'

He was hurriedly mixing rose madder, rose dore and alizarin red, creating a vivid pink on his palette.

She watched him for a time before she said, 'You need to confess the truth, Father.'

He dabbed his brush in the paint.

'I know what you have done. I found the crib and the poor infant, the dog and the brooch. I know you have been following me. I know all these things.'

She waited. But still he did not respond and she reached and took the brush from his hand. 'If you are trying to hurt me –' She stopped and looked into his face.

174

He took another brush from the jar and continued applying paint to the canvas.

'This is about you, Father – your soul. Tell me, no, tell God what you have done.' She took a deep breath and held it until her chest hurt.

He continued working.

'Is this the way you would have it? Can you not sense the danger? Can you not smell it in the air? You are smelling Hell, Father,' she whispered.

'I am working!' he snapped.

'I believe you have murdered two human beings. And I also believe you may not even know what you have done. You may be quite ill, Father. If I am right, you must try to focus your mind, confess your sins and beg forgiveness of God. Or face damnation.'

She chewed on her lower lip until she tasted blood and then turned back to the hacienda. She froze.

Aba was standing a few feet away in the shadows, the old servant glaring at her through the darkness. 'He did not do these things!' she snapped, turning and marching back into the house.

Don Lugo chuckled.

Sister Ria waited until Aba had disappeared into the house and then she looked back at her father and shouted, 'Tell me!'

The Patrón pulled the cowl off his head and looked at her and raised his eyebrows. 'Calm yourself, child – wrath is the devil's web.' He had shaved his head and was bleeding in places from the razor, looking like some martyred saint. But he was no saint in her eyes.

'Where is your holy priest?' he mocked.

Sister Ria turned back to the darkened house and saw Aba looking down at her from an upstairs window. There

175

was something frightening in the old woman's look.

'Your priest?' Don Lugo asked again.

Sister Ria turned back to her father. 'This isn't about priests. And if you won't let it be about your soul, then it's about nothing.'

He dismissed her with a wave of his hand. 'You had responsibilities –' His voice broke up into a smoker's hacking cough.

'To God.' She jammed the brush she was holding back into the jar on his easel, splashing paint thinner on him, and stood glaring at him in the lantern light. 'To God,' she hissed. She picked up a rag near his chair and wiped her hands clean.

He returned to his painting.

Sister Ria continued to watch him, recalling the night it had happened, her hands twisting the rag she held. She was shaking – growing increasingly frightened by her inability to stop fragments of yesterdays from flooding in on her, mixing with the present like silt from an overflowing river. Her mind seemed determined to scourge these sharp remembrances for all time, to drag her hatred of him from the shadowed depths of her soul into the harsh light.

The memory danced like a phantasmagoria before her.

She was sitting in the library, staring at the blackened wall of fire bricks lining the massive walk-in fireplace, and trying to remember her dead mother's face in the shadows, her head pounding. Her father was marching back and forth in front of her dressed in a Mexican cavalry officer's uniform with riding pants and knee-high boots and small silver spurs.

He stopped pacing and looked at her. 'You will do as I have said.'

It was close to midnight and candlelight danced slowly on the walls.

'I will not,' she said.

Don Lugo started walking again, like an actor on a stage. 'I would not have decided this had it not been for your foolishness.'

'Foolishness?'

'With Father André.'

'Marrying God is not foolishness, Father.'

'Do not say that again!' he yelled. Then he walked on and composed himself. 'You will marry Don Lorenzo Cortés. It has been arranged. There are —'

'No, Father,' she interrupted.

'You will marry —'

'Do not risk your reputation on it,' she interrupted.

'He is waiting in your room. Go to him.'

She laughed.

'You will be cared for,' he continued. 'La Cienega will be cared for.'

Isadora's eyes were locked on her father's face and she was nodding in a nonsensical way as if agreeing with his every word. She looked away to the dying fire. Her head was hurting and she massaged her temples with the tips of her fingers. 'I am done here, Father.'

'You will not leave until I say you can. You will not turn your back on your responsibilities. Do you understand?'

She continued to watch the embers of the fire, crying softly.

'Don Lorenzo will make a decent husband. Go to him.'

'I am done, Father.'

'You will stay with him this night!'

'This is not the breeding of cattle, Father. Such things

*are not to be done without the sanctification of the Church
and God, and not without love.'*

'You will do it – or I will dismiss the old woman!'

*Instinctively, he had found the one place in her heart
not hardened by calluses. Aba had become a mother to
her. He knew that.*

Isadora Victorine Lugo was gone the next morning.

But she would always remember that night . . .

'You're shaking, child,' he mocked now. 'Surely you are
not afraid of your own father?'

'I shake for your sins,' she said, starting back to the
house.

'Nun,' he called after her.

She turned back. 'Yes?'

'It belongs to me,' he said, pointing at the rag.

She sailed it into the night sky.

Determined not to think about her past in this house, she
lay in her bed listening to the wind in the garden. The
room felt cold and she was shivering. She rolled onto her
side and pulled the covers up to her neck.

Sister Ria was dozing when someone tried the handle
of the garden door. She bolted upright and held her breath
and watched as they tried a second time, the heavy brass
bar lowering slowly. Then they pressed against the thick
wood. The lock held.

She was instantly awake.

Moments later she saw a shadow at the shutters and
heard pressure being applied to them as well. Also locked.
She slipped out of bed and tiptoed to the door and peeked
out through a thin gap into the night. Nothing. Badly
frightened, she pressed against the wall of her bedroom
and waited, the wind stirring the bushes outside her room

178

and whining softly through the eaves of the house.

Whoever it was, they were waiting as well. There was no way they could know for certain whether she was asleep or awake. Her eyes searched for a weapon. She shook her head: God was her weapon. As if her thoughts had reached them, there came a soft knock on the garden door. She pressed harder against the wall, afraid to speak.

A voice, rushed and frightened, said, 'Let me in.'

Sister Ria took a step forward, then halted. The voice could belong to Cristina or Estrella or one of the other servants. Had her father tried to harm another woman? The words had been badly strained – but so had the voice in the alley. Her heart sped. She waited, flattened against the wall of the bedroom.

The voice came muffled through the thick wood again. 'Sister Ria. Please let me in. I'm hurt.' She could hear sobbing.

Unable to ignore the pleas for help, she moved quickly to the door before she realized it was locked. 'Wait while I find the key.' She turned in the dark and stepped around Estrella's empty bed, the girl was on kitchen duty. Sister Ria felt over the top of her night stand for the heavy key, picked it up and hurried back.

She had just inserted it into the lock when she saw the bronze lever being pushed slowly down again – not rushed or panicked. She froze. A voice in her mind kept screaming 'No!'

Sister Ria stepped back. 'Who are you?'

Silence.

Then the voice said, 'Open the door.' It was a demand now.

Sister Ria did not open her door. She ran from her room, down the hallway to the back of the hacienda and

Aba's quarters. The old woman wasn't there, and Sister Ria hurried down the dark passage to her father's room and banged on his door. There was no response there either. Then she thought she heard something and pressed closer to the door.

'Father?'

From behind her, a voice said, 'May I help you?'

She whirled and peered into the darkness of the hallway. Someone was standing near the library door, a dark figure almost lost in the thick shadows. Then they started walking toward her. Sister Ria was backing away, when she realized that it was the Patrón. He was no longer wearing the monk's cowl.

'I asked you a question, nun.'

She did not answer. Instead, she studied his clothing, a black cape and shirt, black pants and boots, and on his head, a black gaucho hat of the kind that the police had found at the murder scene. She shuddered.

'Where have you been?' she asked.

He said nothing.

'Someone tried to get into my room. I was worried they had broken into your bedroom.'

'How very touching,' he said, unlocking his door.

'Were you just in the garden?' she asked.

He stepped inside his room and closed the door.

'Tell me!'

He did not.

Sister Ria trotted down the hall to the rear of the hacienda and pounded on Aba's door again. When there was still no response, she ran to the kitchen, where she found Min and Estrella and the old man who served as the hacienda's night watchman, all three asleep.

She shook them awake and with lighted lamps and Min

180

carrying the kitchen's meat cleaver and the old man an ancient pistol that looked like it might be far more dangerous to him than anyone else – they searched the courtyard and the gardens for the intruder. Fernando joined them, stalking ahead as they moved through the night.

They found no one.

Sister Ria was pacing anxiously back and forth in the narrow passage in front of Aba's apartment, waiting for the woman to return. Min and the others had returned to the kitchen at the far end of the hacienda, and would not venture out into the living quarters again that night unless summoned.

Aba, where are you?

Fear building in her, she tried the woman's door.

Open.

Fernando shot inside and hopped up onto the small bed and sat. Sister Ria turned in a slow circle and looked at the sparsely furnished compartment, small and filled with nothing but a bed, a chest of drawers, a table and chair. She struggled with a numbing thought taking shape in her mind, trying to avoid it.

She could not. The voice outside her bedroom and in the alley could both have been Aba's. 'Impossible,' she whispered and started to leave. Then she stopped. It was not impossible. She began to search through the small room.

Minutes passed slowly, until Sister Ria was done. She had poked through everything in the room, hunting for the book of poems or the brown suit, the black fedora, anything that might implicate the old servant. All the while, she had prayed that she would find nothing. And she had not.

181

She was on her knees taking one more look under the mattress, and feeling greatly relieved, when she saw Fernando hop down and walk to the door, his ears forward, staring intently at the crack at the bottom. She quickly stood and focused on the doorknob, the old cat continuing to watch the crack. Her heart was pounding. Was the intruder still in the house? Was he on the other side of the door? Sister Ria stepped forward and yanked the door open. Aba stood gazing at her.

Neither of them spoke. Then the old woman looked past her at the things disturbed in her small room.

'I've looked everywhere for you, Aba.' She paused. 'Someone tried to break into my room. I thought perhaps you had been harmed.'

'I was at the river,' she said, her eyes moving past Sister Ria to her room again.

'I'm sorry, Aba. I had to know,' she said quickly.

'Had to know?'

'Whether or not you had the book.'

The old servant looked into her face for a moment, 'You mean whether I had killed that woman?'

Sister Ria looked down at the floor.

'And did you find it?'

Sister Ria shook her head.

'So then I am not a murderer?'

'Oh Aba, I never really believed –' Sister Ria stopped as if the words had been yanked from her mouth. Aba was holding the little book out to her.

'Is this what you were searching for?'

Sister Ria couldn't find her voice. The book was the companion volume to the one in her pocket. Aba continued to hold it out to her.

'Take it.'

182

Sister Ria did not.

'I assume you are revising your grand murder theories yet again.'

'Where did you find it? I searched his room.'

'Are you now back to blaming your father? For the first time in my life I am ashamed of you, Isadora.' Aba tossed the book onto the bed. 'It was in plain sight on a table in the sitting room. I picked it up after I found you searching for it in the library and have carried it in my pocket since – knowing if you found it you would simply blame him again for that woman's murder, and stop searching. Which, of course, you are doing right now.' She looked into Sister Ria's face. 'Unless you have decided I'm a murderer.'

'I had hoped it belonged to someone other than my father, Aba.'

'That is a lie, Isadora.' Aba continued to watch her for a second and then said, 'Leave my room, please.'

'I'm sorry.'

'Leave.'

FIVE DAYS . . .

She t..........

Mother h..........

India like it were the........

FIFTEEN

All night long Sister Ria had been thinking about Aba and Dorothy Regal, sitting in a rocking chair on the veranda, aching from the worry and fatigue. Over and over she told herself the old servant was not a murderer. How she knew didn't matter. She just knew. But she could not say the same for her father. She was certain that the night before he had tried to get into her room from the garden.

As she sat telling herself this, she heard wheels over sand and looked up to see the morning stagecoach rolling down the long winding drive. It stopped in front of the house, and she gave up thinking about the two women and sat watching as the driver crawled down and began removing boxes from the boot of the coach. Fernando was sitting next to her.

The man worked without saying anything. Then he brought her a box from the coach and said, 'That's all of them.'

She pulled on her glasses and read the label.

Mother Superior Isabel at the Benedictine convent in India liked to quote the seventeenth-century English poet

William Cowper: *Sometimes a light surprises the Christian while he sings; it is the Lord who rises with healing in his wings.* And as she watched the driver walking back to the stage, Sister Ria found herself quoting Cowper.

She heard a door close behind her, and she stood and turned around. The Patrón was standing on the veranda wearing a US cavalry officer's brown jacket over his night shirt, and holding a stiff salute to the brim of an old campaign hat. Then he snapped to parade-rest like some ancient warrior.

Sister Ria was still looking at her father when the driver asked, 'Who's signing for these?'

She just stood staring at her father.

'Hey, lady, I got other stops. You want these or not – seventy-five boxes of kids' shoes and socks? What are you running, an orphanage?' The man looked at the box in his hand. 'This one says: Ortho-po –'

'Orthopedic,' she mumbled.

He had bought shoes for the orphans. He was about to die and he had ordered the children shoes. One, a corrective shoe for Estrella. Sister Ria could not take her eyes off his face.

That night, she stood on the sidewalk in front of the candle shop in town where she had just purchased thirteen white votives for her father's wake and looked down at the open telegram in her hand. Suddenly her tongue thrust forward and she felt sick.

She gazed down at the words on the page, her head pounding. Clemente Rojo had surprised her by delivering the message that afternoon, saying he had happened to be in the telegraph office when it came through. She reread it now for the hundredth time. 'Governor will not help. Leave. Danger. Millie.'

Sister Ria shook her head. She would not leave.

Five days.

She pulled the piece of paper that she had found in Dorothy Regal's room from her pocket and studied it once again – recalling what the curandera's niece had said: 'The woman was being followed.'

She was being followed as well.

She started to walk. Fernando strolled along behind her – the old cat ever faithful. The bell in the Plaza church rang nine times.

The American section of town looked shut down for the night and so she headed to the plaza district. Unlike Main Street, La Calle del Negro was packed with people. The night was hot and dry, the street filled with a jarring cacophony of piano and organ music, laughter and shouting. She studied the faces of those who passed her on the sidewalk, hunting for the little man in the brown suit. Or better, hoping he was hunting her. She was convinced that if she found him she would find her father. And have the final proof that she needed to be rid of the doubt in her. She had started this search for answers because of Aba and her mother but now she knew she was searching for herself.

When she did not find him on La Calle del Negro, she headed for the plaza.

She made a slow circuit around the perimeter of the gardens, trying to act as if she were simply taking the night air. She stopped and picked a handful of white daisies by the path, then waited for a time under the light of one of the gas lamps, knowing that she was clearly visible in the yellow glow, watching the night around her for the figure of the man. Fifteen minutes later, she began walking the perimeter path again. No one was out in the night. Worse, no one followed her – so she turned into the darkness of the gardens, making herself a more enticing target, moving slowly down a path that cut diagonally through the shrubs and trees towards the Pico Hotel. She lingered for a time in the night near the old limestone fountain in the centre of the grounds, trying to sort through the insect sounds for the sound of footsteps, waiting for him to materialize in the darkness. He did not. Where was he? Surely he knew where she was. She watched a possum scurry across the path in front of her, disappearing in a thick stand of lilies, as if he had been swallowed by a green sea. Thirty minutes passed and still he had not shown himself. She moved on – deeper into the dense foliage of the gardens.

Sister Ria sat down on a bench under a dark arbour draped with old wistaria that blocked the moonlight and created a small cave in the darkness. The air was heavy with dew and she pulled her shawl tighter around her shoulders. She waited.

It did not take long this time.

He came down the path slowly, stopping and turning his head back and forth in the night, searching for something. The man's careful movements looked sinister in these dark surroundings. She began to grow nervous, and dropped the daisies she was holding. She gripped the wooden crucifix that she had purchased and attached to her cincture that afternoon. She was frightened. It had been a mistake to have come here. But she had no choice, she told herself. She had to know. Her eyes narrowed in the dim light as she tried to make out the face under the hat. Dressed in her black habit and sitting in the dense darkness under the arbour, she was almost invisible.

As if he could feel her eyes on him, the figure turned slowly on the path until he was staring directly at the arbour. He had still not seen her. He looked confused and turned away again. From the size and shape of the cloaked and hatted figure, she was almost certain it was her father. Suddenly overcome with anger, she stood up from the bench.

'I'm here, Father,' she snapped, 'do you want to kill me?'

The figure whirled. And Sister Ria took a step back and sat down hard on the bench. It was not her father.

Clemente Rojo seemed to force a smile. He was holding his little silver gun in one hand.

'Good Sister,' he said, tipping his head, still smiling. 'Praise God you're OK.'

'You were following me,' she said.

'Yes.'

'Why?'

'I saw you walking alone around the plaza. It's not safe.'

'I grew up in this pueblo,' she said stiffly.

'Yes, but Los Angeles is now a dangerous place.' He stepped into the darkness of the arbour, blocking her exit to the path, the little silver pistol at his side. 'People are murdered in these gardens. I would not want that to happen to you.' The smile had left his face.

Sister Ria's heart was thumping against the wall of her chest, remembering that he had brought her Milagros' telegram. And now he was here, following her in the dark. 'You carry a pistol –'

'Yes, Los Angeles is a dangerous place,' he repeated softly, stepping even closer to her.

Sister Ria stood up and said, 'I must go. Don Vargas is waiting for me at the hotel. I'm sure he is looking for me now.'

'You must be mistaken. Don Vargas is at his home. Resting. He is an old man.'

'No, he is waiting for me,' she lied.

'You sound frightened.'

'You startled me, that's all.'

She took a step forward. Clemente did not move to the side to let her pass. She was about to step around him when she heard the sound of voices in the darkness and the editor turned and watched as a young couple strolled down the path. Sister Ria didn't hesitate. She walked out of the arbour and trailed closely behind the man and woman until she reached Olive Street. Clemente had strolled along at a distance behind them.

'Good night, Sister,' he called, 'and be safe.'

Sister Ria hurried to La Calle del Negro, shaken by her encounter with Clemente Rojo. Had he truly just stumbled upon her by accident as she walked around the plaza, as he had said, or had he been following her? There seemed to be too many coincidences connected to him. Was he somehow involved? Millie had told her to trust no one. Still, he could simply be a newspaper man out at night walking around looking for news, carrying a pistol because the town was indeed dangerous.

She was midway down the street when her heart began to beat faster, thumping against the walls of her chest. Someone was trailing behind her again. She could feel the person. Was it Clemente?

She whirled around to confront him. He was not there. All she saw was three drunks. She searched the crowd with her eyes. Clemente was nowhere to be seen. She walked on, returning to her hunt for the man in the brown suit.

After looking up and down both sides of the street, she turned to the windows, peering into each establishment as she passed, searching the people's faces inside for him. Nothing. Fernando had suddenly joined her. He had probably been having a meal of Italian leftovers. He liked Italian food and had a knack of begging it from the Italian cooks in the old town. The cat trailed quietly along – too quiet, seemingly worried about her. 'I'm fine,' she said to him. He looked up at her then looked away as if he could not care less about her.

Strand's Road was a few yards in front of her – a man was urinating against a brick wall. She turned away and waited for him to finish, then moved into the lighted passageway. While it was not as crowded as La Calle del Negro, there were a number of men and women moving in both directions over its bricked surface. Fernando was no longer following her. She started up the narrow road.

At the top she stopped and took a long, close look at the building. The structure appeared to have once been a handsome home. There was nothing that designated it as a house of prostitution. Just a small black-lettered sign over the front door: La Fiesta. The glass in the windows had been painted black. There were three carriages tied up outside. She forced her thoughts back to the reason she had come: to find her father dressed in the brown suit. She had hoped to find him walking up Strand's Road or standing outside the building. She wasn't about to go looking for him inside. Perhaps if she waited he would come out the door or up the street. It was as good as any other idea she had had.

She leaned back against a brick fence on the opposite side of the road and stood watching the building, mulling over her fears about him, about her life. Standing there and gazing at the side staircase that led to Dorothy Regal's small apartment, Sister Ria wondered if she had missed something in that room. She fought the urge to go back. Then a heavy blanket of fatigue draped over her and she closed her eyes.

The man was on her fast.

He had come out of the shadows and knocked her to the ground with a blow that momentarily dazed her, then dragged her through an open gate into a small fenced enclosure filled with stacks of lumber. She twisted away and scrambled to her feet and started to run, but something collided with her skull and the world was suddenly spinning. Her mind blotted out in a dark haze.

Through the fog drifting behind her eyes, she heard Milagros telling her to move, to get away, and she rolled through a puddle of muddy water, clawing desperately at the dirt, trying to escape. Then someone was ordering her to keep quiet or he would kill her.

The whine started deep in the pit of her.

'Shut up,' the voice snapped, then a fist slammed into her head, the blow driving the side of her face into the dirt. Blood spurted from her nose and the world went silent. The only thing she heard was a small clear voice somewhere deep in her brain: Milagros calling to her to play. It was warm and sunny . . . and safe.

He had her on her back. She slid into dark nothingness.

When she came to, she thought she had been buried alive, before she realized it was worse: her habit had been pulled over her head and hands were yanking at her undergarments.

'I am Christ's bride!' she shouted.

The man straddling her chest butted her with his head,

the blow splitting her lip. She clawed at his head and tried to bite him through the material of her habit.

'You will not touch me, do you understand? God will curse you for all eternity!' she yelled. He slapped her.

'I told you to shut up,' he hissed. 'You should have left like your sister.'

Sister Ria froze. He was part of this, involved in it – he knew. She struggled harder but the man was too heavy and strong. Then there was the sound of people running up the alley and lantern light bouncing in the night, and the man straddling her chest leaped away into the darkness.

When she had finally gained control over the spasms in her body, Sister Ria looked down at the mud covering her habit and made a weak attempt to get it off, then her legs went out from under her. For a time, the small crowd of men just stood and watched her sitting, her arms and legs akimbo, looking badly out of sorts.

She stared up into their faces.

'You okay, Ma'am?' one of the men asked.

She nodded, but didn't move. Two of them helped her to her feet and walked her slowly out to the front of the brothel. The crowd was respectfully quiet. Finally one of them asked, 'You got a carriage somewhere, Ma'am?' She just gazed into the man's face.

Then someone pulled a black canvas-topped carriage up in front of her and said, 'I'll take her home.'

She was wobbling on her feet and the men struggled to politely push her up into the back seat, then they pulled the curtains closed around her. 'You sure you're okay?' one of the men asked, sticking his head in through the split in the side curtain. 'We can get a doctor, if you want.'

She shook her head no and wiped blood from her nose

and then leaned back into the seat and closed her eyes. There was a curtain separating her from the driver and she listened as he clucked once and the little carriage horse started up Strand's Road, away from the brothel and La Calle Del Negro. They drove a couple of miles without talking.

The night was hot and dry until a rain squall blew in from the Pacific, the water pounding hard on the canvas roof. Sister Ria's head was clearing and she focused on the sound of the pelting rain. The overhang of the carriage roof would cover the driver, but she knew from experience that the downpour, driven by the wind, would be getting into where the man sat. 'I'm sorry about the rain,' she called through the curtain. If he responded, she did not hear him.

Near the edge of town, a little black dog yapped at the carriage from the sagging veranda of a small adobe house. A large Mexican who looked like he'd been drinking stumbled out onto the porch to see who was bothering his dog. 'Silencio,' the man hollered belligerently at the passing carriage, then he went back inside.

'Thank you for taking me home,' she said to the driver, through a small crack in the curtain. The man said something this time but in the rain Sister Ria could not make the words out. She ran a finger over her teeth and jaw and cheek bones so see that nothing was broken. There wasn't. Finished, she looked around her in the darkness of the cabin, her eyes focusing on a small brass plaque on one of the doors that read, 'Bradford's Livery'. The carriage was rented. That seemed odd to her.

Sister Ria was about to offer money to cover the rental, when her nose began to bleed again. She tipped her head back and called out to the driver, 'Pardon me. Do you

have some paper or a rag I can use to stop a nose-bleed?'
She listened as the man pulled the canvas tool bag from
under the seat and began to look through it. Then the
road suddenly became rougher, the carriage hitting ruts
and rocks, and she glanced out the side curtain. They had
taken a wrong turn and were headed for the foothills of
the Santa Monica mountains.

Before Sister Ria could say anything, the driver stuck
his arm back inside the cabin and she froze. Her mouth
was opening and shutting in silent gasps. It was the sleeve
of a brown suit. The realization hammered at her like a
fist, panic and confusion whirling inside her. Her hands
were shaking so badly that she could barely control them.
She took the rag and immediately dropped it. Then she
heard the sound. It was the same sound she had heard in
the darkness of her bedroom: a hard metallic snap.

Seconds later, the arm came slashing back through the
curtain, the long blade of a knife slicing through the air,
catching material and cutting deeply through the leather
seat. Moments later, the driver yanked the curtains aside
and stared at the empty cabin.

The side door was open.

FOUR DAYS . . .

SIXTEEN

Sister Ria had been afraid to sleep in the hacienda and had hidden herself in the garden and stayed up most of the night watching the house. She saw no one. As dawn broke, she slept.

And she dreamed.

She was stumbling through a dark room filled with the sharp smell of incense. People were following her, grasping at her in the night. She turned and ran outside the room down a long stone corridor, panic growing, footsteps behind her. They were gaining on her when she turned into a second room and slammed a heavy wooden door shut. She stood catching her breath and listening for them. Whoever they were, they were gone. Then she sensed that she was not alone in the room and she turned slowly around.

The woman was young and beautiful, with a sweet child nursing at her breast. The woman smiled at her and she was certain in that glorious moment that she was looking into the face of the Virgin Mother. Then the child in the Madonna's arms turned its head and gazed at her with a gentleness that soothed her troubled soul.

*Sister Ria was on her knees when the child spoke,
the heavy sound of its voice causing her to jump. 'Sister
Ria –'*

'Yes, Lord?'

'You must not help him –'

'Why, Lord?'

'He is damned.'

She said nothing.

*'Nun – do you understand? You must think of your
own soul and not do the bidding of the wicked. It will
not go well with you if you do.' The child watched her
for a long moment, then said, 'Do you understand me?'*

She nodded.

*The child smiled and then went back to nursing at his
mother's breast, his eyes on Sister Ria.*

Sister Ria screamed herself awake in the bright morning
sunlight. She couldn't recall having felt like this in her life:
absolutely unable to think clearly. Had she seen a vision
of the Virgin and the Christ Child? Had her Lord truly
warned her to do nothing to save her father? She hurried
down the long loggia toward her father's room, listening
to the sounds of things being moved, of clanging and
banging.

Rounding the corner, she jerked to a halt. The wide
hallway outside her father's room was a jumbled mess of
furniture, personal belongings, pails, brooms and mops.
Servants were hurrying in and out of the room, carrying
the pens of animals that Sister Ria had just had the servants
remove two days before. Her father must have ordered
them returned during the night. He would never give up
on anything. Aba was just as stubborn and Sister Ria could
hear the old head servant giving orders, busily enforcing
the new rules of cleanliness.

Don Maximiato was sitting in a large leather chair in the middle of the hallway, dressed in a Turkish bathrobe, a fez with a long black tassel stuck on top of his head, the tassel falling in front of his face. He slapped at it like it was an annoying fly.

'You treat me as if I am a child,' he yelled.

Aba appeared in the doorway looking sternly down at the old man. 'Only when you do not cooperate, Don Lugo. It is for your own good. The room is filthy again. The animals are not good for your health.'

Min appeared, wearing a beautiful red silk Chinese robe, the long wide sleeves rolled up, a green ribbon tied in his pigtail. He was carrying a stack of papers that he set down at Aba's direction on the hallway floor then he quickly returned to the room. He looked sad, as if he was the only one who realized what was about to happen.

Then Don Lugo suddenly began giggling. Aba watched him for a moment, then shook her head and disappeared back into the room. The Patrón leaned back and shut his eyes, something lizard-like in his look.

She knelt beside him. 'Father. Listen to me.' While her Lord might not want her to save him, he could save himself. Perhaps that had been the Christ Child's message: he must save himself . . . no one could do it for him. He was facing death and must repent his sins. That was what mattered now.

'Father.'

He opened one eye.

'The time is near.'

He tipped his head and looked at her clothing. 'Why do you dress like that?'

'Because I am a nun.'

203

'No – to annoy me.' He licked his lips with a careful pass of his tongue. 'Have you checked the fields, the ewes in the breeding barn?'

She shook her head. 'None of that matters any more.'

'I didn't think you had.'

'Father, your time is almost at hand. You must not allow yourself to be taken unawares.'

He smiled an odd twisted smile and leaned over and touched the top of her veil. Then he pressed his thumb into her forehead and made the sign of the cross on her skin. 'Do you wish me to pray for you?'

'No, Father. Pray for yourself.'

He said nothing, just turned and picked up a cigarette from a small table and lit it on a burning candle, continuing to stare at her face.

She sat back, shaking her head in sadness. 'Is there anything I can do for you?'

He picked a piece of ash from the tip of his tongue and then took another draw on the cigarette and blew a cloud of smoke into her face. 'Trade me your outfit. I have made you a perfectly good offer.'

Sister Ria stood, tears welling in her eyes. Not even the closeness of his own death could frighten him into reality. 'You must seek absolution. You must do this for yourself. I cannot help you.'

He said nothing.

'That is all I can do for you – tell you to save your soul. At least do that, please.'

'I thought you wanted to save my soul yourself.'

'I cannot –'

The old plaza church looked very different. Sister Ria gazed up at a European-style belfry that had been added onto one side of the edifice, steep marble steps rising in front of her, leading to heavy carved double doors. There was something off-putting about these changes.

To her left stood a tall adobe wall, some thirteen feet high, covered with a veneer of fresh white plaster: *the garden wall of saints.* She went through its open doorway into an enclosed courtyard with formal pathways, fountains and dark hidden pockets amidst lush greens.

She moved slowly through the beautiful garden listening to the splashing of water, smelling the rich tang of orange blossoms and feeling that the humble old church and this exquisite garden did not belong together. She pulled on the heavy sanctuary door and slipped inside – reluctant in a way she understood but didn't want to face. The church reminded her of the small medieval cathedrals in the southern regions of Spain, beautiful in its stark simplicity. It had been built in 1822 with crude tools and simple materials by the tireless labour of Franciscan Indian neophytes. The church of her childhood – but like everything else in her life, forever changed.

The high ceiling was still supported by the same dark rough-hewn beams, but now there were lovely brass chandeliers hanging from the central beam, and the thick walls gleamed a stark bone white from fresh plaster. The altar was new and built of beautiful gleaming woods, replacing the rough adobe platform of her youth. The rows of benches were also gone, instead there were oak pews padded with red velvet cushions. Even the old uneven floor had been replaced by a level layer of heavy red tile polished to a brilliant sheen.

The rough wooden plaques in Spanish commemorating the Stations of the Cross that as a child Sister Ria had lovingly run her hands over a thousand times were now beautiful white marble slabs, the sacred words chiselled in English into the cold hard stone. She stared at the Christ on the Cross and wondered again if He and the Virgin had truly come to her in the vision of her dream. If they had, was she violating Christ's warning? She shook her head. Surely he would let her father confess his sins and save himself. She knelt and clasped her hands in front of her face: 'I will not help him, Lord,' she moaned softly. 'I leave that to you.'

She began to cry.

Sister Ria was praying when a door opened at the rear of the sanctuary and a tall, thin padre in a beautiful white cassock, a silver crucifix dangling from his corded waist, appeared with a well-dressed American woman at his side. They were deep in conversation about a wedding, the priest laughing at something the woman had said, and he did not notice her at first as they approached down the aisle towards her. The priest was smoking a cigarette, his accent French, his English excellent.

The priest saw her first and stopped and looked at her as if surprised that anyone would stand in this church without his permission. The American woman continued on, then stopped and looked back at her.

'May I help you?' the priest asked in Spanish. His tone was quietly arrogant.

It seemed an odd question of a priest to a nun of his faith. The man's pale face was screened in a thin veil of smoke.

'Is Father Guevera here?' she asked.

He raised the cigarette to his lips with yellow-stained fingers and took a draw and held it, studying her. He did not look pleased seeing her here. The American woman had given her a passing glance and walked on towards the front doors.

206

'I will be back,' the priest said, hurrying after the woman.

Nervous, Sister Ria watched him. He was perhaps forty but something about him looked much older and he did not look healthy. He talked for a moment to the woman, laughing and gesturing with his hands, then they both looked at her, the woman nodding at something the priest said. After a few more minutes of conversation, the priest kissed her hand and she left.

He returned down the aisle. 'Madrid,' he said to her. 'Father Guevera has been in Madrid for some seven years. He is sick, perhaps dead.' There was no feeling to the words.

'Monsignor Abel?'

'He left this morning for Santa Barbara.'

The man waited for her to say something. When she didn't, he took another pull on what was left of his cigarette and then let it drop to the beautiful floor where he put it out with his sandal. 'You are the Mexican nun. Your father is Maximiato Lugo.'

'Spanish nun. I have come to ask you to hear his confession and to prepare him for death.'

The man waited.

'I lived here in the pueblo once,' she said, feeling awkward. 'This was our church. My grandfather helped construct it, my parents married in it, and I –'

He held up his hand, the gesture indicating that he did not want this conversation with her. 'I have heard of you – of your father.' He paused. 'He has created his own church. He has been convicted of murder. I cannot bless such a man or administer the last rites.'

She glanced around her. 'The sanctuary is very beautiful,' she said, 'different than when I worshipped here.'

'Yes. Now how else may I be of service to you?'

'The Mexican people believe this is no longer their church. That is the reason my father expanded our family chapel. That is not a sin. You must bless him.'

The priest shook his head. 'Is there anything else?'

'You must,' she repeated, more desperate this time. Then a moment later, she added, 'An unborn foetus –'

'I have heard that also,' he said, interrupting her again. 'An unborn stained by sin – never baptized.' He was shaking his head.

'The child needs to be given the last rites of burial as well.'

'Impossible.'

'It is just a child,' she said, emphatically.

'Satan's child.'

'No, just a little unborn child.' Her voice was rising. 'Who never had a chance at the life God had given it. And my father needs to be brought to God at his final hour.'

The priest stood gazing off at the altar as if lost in his own thoughts, then caught himself and looked back at her. 'You, a nun, of all people, should know I cannot sanctify this child's or your father's soul.'

She stared at the heavy golden cross that stood on the altar.

'I suggest you worry about what you believe, nun.'

Sister Ria turned on her heel and walked towards the rear of the church. She turned back. 'Do you know where the child's mother is buried?'

The priest looked surprised. 'You don't?' He lit another cigarette.

'No.'

He took a long draw on the cigarette, blowing the smoke out through his nostrils, and looking pleased with himself.

'Your family cemetery. Making it unholy ground.'

Sister Ria smothered her surprise. 'Thank you.' She started again for the rear of the church.

'Nun,' the man said sharply.

Sister Ria stopped but did not turn around. 'Yes?'

'Stay away from that woman and this unborn creature as well – unless you wish to join your father in damnation,' he said.

'And you may go to Hell as well, priest.'

The candalabrum was burning in her father's bedroom when she knocked and pushed the door open and walked inside. He was dressed in a woman's silk kimono with a bright red obi around his waist, sitting cross-legged on the bed, eyes closed, the palms of his hands turned upwards, his lips moving silently. She waited. The sharp smell of carbolic acid mixing with burning incense filled her nostrils and made her sneeze. If he heard, he did not move.

When he seemed to have stopped praying, she said, 'Father, we must bury the child.'

Sister Ria felt as if she had been struck with a board – a dizzying sickness flowed over her. She could not take her eyes off it. The deep hole had been dug next to her mother's grave. She stood in the fading cadmium light of the California dusk looking down at the dark cavity in the earth, her body trembling. She could hear the familiar sound of a covey of Gambil's quail calling to one another in the chaparral higher up the hillside and thought of the hundreds of times she had walked these same hills with him discussing the crops and livestock of the rancho.

Slowly she gained some control over herself and placed a hand on the cold marble of her mother's gravestone and watched the old women who worked in the kitchen coming up the mountain, their heads draped in black shawls, bearing baskets with roses that they began to place around a smaller hole that had been recently dug a few yards down the hill. The women were moaning and crying and she felt swept up in their melancholy and remembered what Mother Superior Isabel said to her crying sisters each time they buried one of the leper children: 'Your sorrow is God's purpose.'

She had never understood before. She did now.

Her eyes moved to a fresh mound of earth beside the tiny grave. The French priest was at least right about one thing: Dorothy Regal had been buried inside the rock wall of the Lugo family cemetery on the gentle south-facing slope of the hill behind the hacienda. Sister Ria bent and kissed her mother's gravestone and then walked over and put a hand on Dorothy Regal's wooden cross, remembering the priest's warning that the woman was unclean, that she had soiled the sacred burial ground. 'I am glad you are here, Dorothy. May God bless your soul and the soul of your child.'

Peering down at the woman's grave, Sister Ria was struck by the kindness and caring behind the act of bringing this woman whom the Church condemned to Hell, whom the Church would not bury, to this precious place. She would never understand him fully – never quite grasp the great swings of his emotions, the confusing dichotomy of his enormous sensitivity and kindness interspersed with sharp bursts of anger and cruelty.

She gazed out across the fields of La Cienega, across the distant hills to the familiar blue strip of sea and the little island of Santa Catalina looking like the back of a giant lizard in the azure waters. The Lugo cemetery had been chosen and sanctified 100 years before by her great grandfather, Rialto Miguel Francisco Lugo, and the pueblo priest – chosen so that Don Rialto's young wife, Maria, dead bearing Sister Ria's grandfather, Raúl Simón Lugo, would always face the shimmering sea she loved, the sea she had prayed would some day take her home to her beloved Spain.

Since that blessed day of sanctification, every member of the Lugo family of Alta California had been buried here. She felt the stubbornness rise in her breast. The ground was not unclean. It was holy ground and would always be so – and Dorothy Regal and her child were welcome.

The women had finished placing the roses around the edge of the tiny grave, when the others arrived. It was a solemn procession. Don Lugo came first, wearing a spotless white satin alb fringed in purple and gathered at the waist – the mitre of a Catholic bishop on his head. He walked slowly, carrying a long wooden staff tipped with a golden cross; three young Indian boys following him in the brown robes and straw sandals of acolytes. Sister Ria smiled. There was something very right about the procession – sanctified or not. Then she saw Auel carrying a beautiful miniature rosewood coffin, the size of a shoe box, in his old hands, and she clasped her hands in front of her. Min, Estrella and Cristina and the other mourners followed the old man. Aba was not among them.

The service was not long. Her father conducted it in the ancient Latin text of the Church. She knew the sacred words of the commitment of the dead to the earth by heart and wondered where he had learned them in such wonderfully precise form. He stood before the small grave, the little coffin resting on a bed of white roses, and spoke the

211

hallowed words crisply and with a depth of feeling that reached deep into her heart, surprising her greatly.

The man possessed a grand theatrical side, she told herself, then shook her head. Whatever he did, be it addleheaded or cruel, he passionately believed. His blessing, his curse. She listened to the old Roman words spilling out into the dry air, drifting through the evening light as if they might drift on forever. Even to God.

It was almost dark, the ceremony at a close. She watched as he bent and placed his hands on the coffin, sweat running down his face. Gently, he patted the wood as if touching the head of a living child. 'Lord, we commend this sinless soul to your forgiving grace. Joyous that she will grow up in your Heaven.' Sister Ria was smiling through her tears and nodding. Then Auel and Min began to lower the little coffin into God's hands.

She continued to watch him. The final words had been his words, not those of the church. And they had been exactly right – words the priest at the plaza church should have spoken here. Sister Ria walked to his side. He was gazing into the grave and she wondered what he saw, whether he was seeing his own life spilling down into the earth, at last coming to grips with his approaching end.

'Father?'

He continued looking down.

'Thank you,' she said.

He did not respond.

Auel removed the purple cloth from the child's headstone, folded it carefully and handed it to one of the women, then placed the bottom edge of the small marble tablet into a slit in the earth at the head of the grave. She took a deep breath and exhaled slowly. Her father had

212

thought of everything that was right and good. Sister Ria crossed herself and stepped forward and knelt before the stone and looked at its smooth surface.

Her eyes moved quickly over the chiselled letters, then back again. She gasped for air. The inscription read:

Isadora Victorine Lugo
1855–1872

She whirled to face him but he was walking away. The boy, Min, was at his side carrying a large black bag. She turned back to the grave. His insane cruelty would damn him, she told herself, her eyes locked on the date chiselled into the smooth surface of the stone: 1872, the year she had fled. She was crying now and running after him.

'How dare you!'

Min jumped away from him when she shouted and held the black bag nervously in both hands, staring at her as though she was mad.

'Your insane games mean nothing to me. But to demean the child? Have you no decency?'

Don Lugo stopped walking and looked back at her.

'You put my name on the child's gravestone!'

He raised his eyebrows. 'Your name? Isadora Victorine Lugo?'

She cleared her throat. 'You know what I mean.'

'Your name is something silly like Sister Lea. Is it not?'

She ignored him.

'The Isadora Victorine Lugo I knew died in 1872 – just as the stone reads.'

'I did not die.'

'And you are not Isadora Victorine Lugo.' He crossed

213

himself, mockingly. He turned and continued to walk slowly down the service road.

Don Lugo spent the next two hours doctoring the sick – poor Mexicans and Indians – who stood lined up in front of the empty work sheds, the sheds serving as temporary examining rooms, and for the sickest patients as wards with small beds. Sister Ria watched him work, silently fuming. Min had helped him into a clean white doctor's smock, tying his priestly cincture and crucifix around his waist, and he was moving quickly and efficiently through the line of waiting patients, listening with a stethoscope to one man's chest, peering into mouths, eyes and ears, probing with his fingers. Grudgingly, she began to sense that his medical technique and decisions were as good as those of the doctors she had worked with over the years in India.

Wounds were properly cleaned and sutured using the latest accepted procedures, teeth pulled, bones set, drugs administered. How, she didn't know, but he had obviously trained himself to understand the body and medicine, the available pharmacology. She thought of the small book on dissection. It made sense now. And she could see that he offered much more than just medicine to these people, administering blessings, brief prayers, advice and coins that Min handed him from the black bag.

The people gazed upon him as though he was truly sainted, and for a moment she understood what Auel had said about him. Then the hurt and anger returned and all thoughts of sainthood dissipated like mist in morning sunlight.

She followed along behind him, angrily looking for a chance to re-engage him in verbal battle. But as the line of the waiting sick and injured grew, something tugged at her heart and she gave up wanting to fight him and joined in the work. Quickly she separated those most seriously ill from the others, leaving the first for him and moving by herself through the rest. He did not object – except to have Min give her a smock to wear. When she finished with her group of patients, she joined him, preparing medicines as he directed, bandaging and cleaning wounds. They worked silently side by side for three more hours. They hadn't worked side by side in ten years. Oddly, she thought, it felt right somehow. And slowly sadness replaced her anger.

It was dark and growing late, the rooms lit by lanterns and candles. They had seen the last patient and the kitchen maids were bringing trays of food and drink and setting them on tables in front of the work rooms. Two young Mexican women dressed as nurses in clean uniforms were helping those who needed help to eat and drink. Min was asleep on one of the beds.

Her father rested on a bench, holding a cigarette in his thin hand, squinting against the drifting smoke. She leaned against a wall, sipping chilled orange juice from a glass and watching him. She had no idea what to think about this man. Perhaps what she had once believed was madness was simply delusion. Whatever his illness, he vacillated between warped illusions of reality and crystal-clear lucidity. She no longer hated him. She wasn't certain what she felt. Pity, perhaps.

Don Maximiato looked up when Sister Ria's shadow fell across him. 'Are there more?'

'No, Father. We are done.'

He nodded and took a pull on his cigarette, then broke into a hacking cough.

When he finally stopped, she said, 'Please –'
'No.'

Sister Ria nodded and sat down on the bench, leaned back into the wall and closed her eyes, exhausted.

The little boat was drifting slowly in the pond water; Isadora lying on her back in the warm afternoon sunshine, a hand dragging in the cool liquid. She had come out with Millie who sat fishing at the other end of the old rowboat. Isadora had never liked to fish, had hated watching the poor creatures desperately flipping on the bottom of the boat, drowning in the air. But Millie loved to fish and so Isadora had joined her. She could hear the old Mexican laundresses gossiping on the shore as they washed clothes in the stream water that fed the pond.

Isadora was still listening to the women when she felt the end of the boat dip down, as if Millie had suddenly stood up. 'Don't, Millie,' she said, remembering the day the summer before when Millie had stood up and tipped them over into the water. The boat continued to rock and Sister Ria came slowly out of her dream and sat up in her bed. She opened her eyes in the darkness of her bedroom, and fought off a scream.

Her father was standing on the bed gazing down at her in the dark. He was wearing a heavy black caftan and holding a knife in one hand at his side, his other hand stuck in the folds of his robe.

She scooted back against the headboard. 'Father?'

He stood silent, staring straight into her face. Yet, she wasn't certain that he even saw her, such was the blankness in his eyes.

'Father, what are you doing?'

216

He neither spoke nor appeared to have heard her. There was no anger, no hatred in his look, just a cold stare.

He took a step forward, the bed rocking.

'Father, speak to me.'

She was trembling now.

'Father?'

Sister Ria was readying herself to flee from the bed, when Aba came hurrying into the room.

'There you are, Don Lugo. Shame on you, disturbing everyone – walking around in your sleep again,' she said quietly, her voice soothing. Aba reached up and took the old man by the arm and slowly turned him toward her. Then carefully, talking gently as she worked, she started to ease the knife from his grasp but he yanked away and turned back to Sister Ria.

'Don Lugo,' the old woman said firmly, and grasped the Patrón again and helped him down from the bed and led him from the room.

Sister Ria was drenched in sweat.

THREE DAYS . . .

SEVENTEEN

José Vargas was sitting in a large leather chair reading a book when a servant brought Sister Ria into the room. The frail old man truly looked like one of God's blessed saints with his gaunt features and long bone-white beard, a brightly coloured Mexican blanket draped across his legs.

Vargas did not look surprised when he saw her standing before him. He motioned her to a nearby chair.

'I didn't know where else to go.'

'You are always welcome.'

'Tell me what to do.'

'Child?'

She took a breath, 'I don't know what to do. You must tell me.'

José Vargas studied her face for a moment, then pulled the hair of his beard and called, 'Antonio.'

The servant reappeared in the doorway. 'Señor Vargas?'

'Café for the good Sister.'

Vargas waited a moment and then said, 'You and your sister have tried very hard.'

Antonio the servant returned carrying a tray with coffee

and sweet cakes which he set on a nearby table. He poured a cup for her.

She waited for him to leave the room.

Vargas just watched her.

Suddenly she looked up at the man as if she had just realized he was in the room and said, 'Don José, you must help me. Please.'

The old man shook his head. 'I am truly sorry.' He seemed to nod off in his chair.

'Don José?'

The old man stirred and sat up straighter and picked up the guitar leaning against his chair, strumming softly, changing chords with his thin fingers, gazing off into the shadows as if remembering other times.

'Don José,' she said more firmly.

He put his hand over the strings and the sound stopped. 'Isadora, you must consider things as they are.'

She waited anxiously for him to continue.

'Your father will die – there is nothing you or I can do for him. You must face that reality.'

She fought to catch her breath. Reality – the word sounded so harsh and cruel.

Don Vargas watched her in the weak light for a time, before he said, 'The offer from the gas company was generous. The Americans control California and the pueblo.'

'I don't care,' she said. 'Tell me you will try to help.'

'You are a beautiful young woman. Take their offer – the money from the sale, along with profits from –'

'Tell me,' she repeated.

'If there are things you do not like in the agreement, I will negotiate changes. Do it, Isadora.'

'Tell me!'

*   *   *

222

It was late evening and the carriage and wagon traffic was beginning to lighten. Sister Ria was moving in a daze down Market Street, her conversation with Vargas replaying itself over and over in her mind. She was suddenly wondering how he fitted into all of this. Could he – her godfather and Don Lugo's closest friend – have helped to condemn the Patrón to death? She gazed down at her hands and continued to mull over what the old man had said.

His persistence that she should sell the land to the gas company troubled her deeply. Slowly, the disturbing thought took full shape in her head: that Don Vargas had sold himself. She fought it off. He could simply be trying to do what was best for her, she told herself. He was, after all, the Lugo family attorney. Perhaps he was only trying to protect her. He had always been a trusted confidant and ally of her father. He could not be his Judas.

She sat down on a nearby bench, struggling against the dark tide of hopelessness rising in her, when she felt someone join her. Sister Ria turned and looked at Chief Hood. The man was holding a mug of hot chocolate that a young Mexican boy had just delivered to him.

'You don't look so well, Miss Lugo.'

'My father is going to die, sir.'

'Because he is a murderer.'

'A man attacked me the other night. Whoever he was, he killed the woman.' Suddenly the warning of the Christ Child flared in her thoughts and she went silent.

Hood asked nothing about the attack. Instead, he said, 'Like some?' raising his cup.

She ignored him.

223

Hood handed the boy a coin and then gazed out at the street as if he were alone.

'Took a while to find you,' he said, finally.

'Truly?' she said sarcastically. 'I thought you knew everything in the pueblo.'

Hood studied her bruised face for a moment, then shook his head. 'I tried to tell you before, Miss Lugo, Los Angeles is not a pueblo, it's an American city.'

'That is a pity, sir.'

'No – it's reality.'

There was that word again. She ignored him.

Hood took a sip of the chocolate. It appeared to burn his lips and he brought the cup down and sat watching the street and blowing on the liquid. Finally, he said, 'Look at that traffic, Miss Lugo. Los Angeles is growing up. Needs sidewalks. More schools. Better fire equipment.' He stopped talking and took another sip.

'Why don't you just say it? Los Angeles needs cheap fuel to run its gas lights.'

He nodded. 'That too.'

'How long have you been on the gas company's payroll?'

Hood stood and touched the brim of his hat. 'I work for the City of Los Angeles, Miss Lugo. For the City and all her people.'

'Not my father –'

'Your father is a murderer, ma'am.'

'You have no proof of that.'

'Have a good day, Miss Lugo. Think about what I've said.' He stood and began walking towards the street.

'May you burn in Hell, sir, if you helped them frame my father.'

Hood ignored her. The Mexican youth who had sold him the chocolate trotted up to retrieve the cup. The man

224

took another drink and handed the cup to the boy. 'You need to calm yourself, ma'am. You don't look well.'

It felt like she was caught in a rock slide, her life crashing down around her, the world closing in on her. Hood was at least right about that: she had to calm down. She lurched from the bench, fear welling inside her. No one to rely on – unless it was Millie. But Millie wasn't here. Thank God for that. She was safe. Sister Ria stumbled forward.

She was moving at a half-run, as if trying to stay ahead of something. It was dark and past supper time and she had just finished hunting the Mexican streets and bars of Los Angeles for the man in the brown suit, the vision of the Christ Child gnawing at her. Over and over again, she prayed for forgiveness. She had to try.

'God, please help me. Give me a sign.'

When no sign came to her, when she could not feel God's presence in her life, she made her decision.

Sister Ria hurried across town and bought a ticket on the Southern Pacific railroad that ran between Los Angeles and Santa Monica. She boarded the train at the railroad terminal on Rives street. Fernando sat quietly on the seat next to her looking as though he would rather be somewhere else. 'Thank you,' she said. The old cat ignored her.

She settled back into her seat. Determined to understand what God wanted her to do. And if God would not come to her, she would go to the place where she had found Him as a child.

There were a few Mexicans moving down the aisle, mostly servants she guessed from their dress and the bundles they carried. They sat in the back of the car gazing out the windows as though they were being sent to prison.

Most of the others who came into the car were Americans, dressed in party clothes, laughing and talking loudly. At other times and places she would have liked the sound of happiness in their voices. But not this night.

Sister Ria stared out the window at the darkened skyline of Los Angeles. She refused to look at her hollow-eyed reflection in the glass, focusing instead on the town. Hood was right: it was no longer a Mexican pueblo, it was an American city of large buildings, mechanical elevators, iron water mains, paved streets, electricity and filament lamps, telephones and 30,000 people. And now she was sitting in one of three fancy rail cars with red leather seats waiting to be taken on an eighteen-minute trip to the bay at Santa Monica – a trip that used to take Millie and her and their nurse-maids half a day on horseback. The change didn't seem possible, not in just eight years.

She had never been to the town of Santa Monica before. It hadn't existed the year she fled the pueblo. It had just been sheep country owned by Francisco Sepulveda – beautiful chaparral-covered hills that rolled down to wide stretches of white sand at the sea's edge. She shook her head at the frightening change. Not just the pueblo. Everything in her life was changing. The familiar was slipping away from her. Worse, she didn't know what she was doing. Was she defying the Christ Child?

She tried again, 'Lord, give me another sign.'

But none came.

She was still looking out the window, past her own reflection in the glass, when she saw it: a quick splash of brown in the crowd on the loading platform. She slid down in her seat, her heart pounding, waiting, trying to see him over the window ledge. She could not. Fernando watched her with his one eye, slowly kneading the leather seat with his front paws.

Sister Ria slid to the floor and started to crawl down the aisle towards the rear door of the rail car, the other passengers stopping their conversations and staring in stunned silence at the nun and the ugly cat that followed her down the aisle. She didn't care how hard they watched, she was going after him. Then the train lurched into motion and she stood up and rushed back to her seat and looked back out the window. He wasn't there.

She sat down and fought the trembling inside her. The man was hunting for her again. Slowly, she began to get the uncomfortable feeling that he was right behind her and she whirled around, surprising two young women sitting behind her. They squealed and she could hear them giggling when she turned back. She ignored them.

Santa Monica was a collection of ramshackle buildings sitting a few hundred yards behind the sandstone bluffs edging the big bay. There was a full moon darting in and out behind small white clouds that looked like sailing ships in the night sky. She stepped down slowly from the train, and waited. She did not see the little man in the crowd. She could smell the ocean. Fernando was close to her.

She pulled her shawl tight around her shoulders and turned in a slow circle. The tiny town was nothing more than a couple of streets of dimly lit beach shanties and shoestring businesses – with a population that couldn't have been more than some seventy-five souls.

When she was a child, people had been drawn here only during the heat of the summers. They came over the hills on horses and buggies, pitched canvas tents under the towering sycamores and stayed for days and weeks,

227

playing games in the surf and sand, lighting bonfires at night to sing and dance by. What could possibly bring this train and all these people here in the dead of night? Then, off in the direction of the ocean, she saw the glow of light in the dark sky.

She moved away from the platform and stood in the shadows of the terminal building watching the other passengers, searching one more time for the man in the brown suit. He was not there. She continued to wait out of sight until the crowd moved on its way, then she turned down a street called Railroad and headed towards the strange yellow glow in the sky. Fernando followed without a sound, which bothered her since he was usually complaining about the condition of his life. She was walking fast, her mind running, her nerves jangled.

Then she froze. Something had moved in the shadows off to her right. She stood and probed the darkness with her eyes. Nothing. But she felt the same shadowed sense of someone watching her. But perhaps she was only making things up in her head.

She walked on.

Her stubbornness securely in place, she felt better. Off to her right, down an impossibly wide boulevard named Ocean Avenue, she saw the lights of a large building. A sign at the corner read: 'Welcome to the Grand Santa Monica Hotel'. She could hear the shrill notes of a calliope splitting the still night air, and smell the sea even more intensely. She had always loved that briny smell of salt and dead sea plants and water – loved this place. Or at least what it had once been. She stopped.

She was standing at the top of the towering bluffs some eighty feet above the sand below. There was a giant wooden staircase that led down – 'The Ninety-Nine Step Staircase',

228

a sign read. But she wasn't looking at the sign or the stairs, she was gazing down at an incredible sight: a broad beach packed with gas-lit bathhouses and restaurants, tented businesses and a large building with red block letters on its clapboard side: 'Santa Monica Beach Pavilion – Hot Steam Baths/Salt Water Plunge'. There was a large wooden pier that ran out into the ocean, lit by colourful lanterns, crowds strolling its length, laughing, children darting and yelling, organs and calliopes playing, the shrill voices of push-cart vendors reaching her in the brisk night air – all of it creating a mad cacophony of discordant sound that after ten years of convent silence was almost frightening to her. Fernando was sitting next to her, his head turning back and forth as he watched the movement below.

It didn't seem possible. She remembered only sand and water and a small work pier that stood to the south called the Shoo Fly. It was gone. Gone also was the beautiful beach, now just rough buildings, a maze of wooden walkways and people.

Her mind was leaping in different directions again. She was recalling other times – good times – when she and Milagros and their governess, Leonora, had ridden down the steep canyon road on their ponies – followed by the ever-present old man, Manuel Escobar, who guarded them as children whenever they left the rancho – to play in the miles of warm sand and surf. Sister Ria tipped her head back and stared up at a million stars and whispered, 'Millie, I love you. I pray you are safe tonight.'

She started down the steep stairs.

She spent the next few hours moving back and forth through the crowds of people, searching for the little man in the brown suit.

She did not find him.

TWO DAYS . . .

EIGHTEEN

The dawn had materialized without her noticing, stealing silently over the beach like a ghost. Sister Ria was sitting in the sand with her knees tucked up under her chin, watching the light break over the ocean, waves exploding in a roaring roll towards the empty shore as if the water would never stop rushing forward. Plovers scurried across the wet sand, fleeing from the on-rushing surge of water, then when it receded they chased after it as if they had lost something valuable in it. She could see the dark smooth heads of sea otters out beyond the breakers – hunting abalone in the rocks below, she figured – and a line of brown pelicans slowly flapping their way north over the surf. Every so often one of the big birds would plunge from the line, diving into the sea as if it had been shot, only to rise flapping out of the foaming waters moments later with a fish in its beak. 'Bless thy creation, Lord,' she whispered.

The shore was empty, stretching miles in both directions; a small driftwood fire burned pleasantly at her back. Fernando was sitting next to her watching the plovers with great interest. He meowed and sat kneading the sand with his front paws. She had not spent the night in this place by accident. It was where God had come to her. But though she had pleaded with her Lord for guidance throughout the night, God had not shown himself to her.

She looked around her at the sand dunes. When she was seventeen her father had brought her here so he could paint. It was the only time they had come here together and she did not know why they had done so.

He had just asked her to accompany him, as if he had something important to say to her. But he had said nothing. He had simply set up his easel and painted all day and into the evening. When he was done, he had handed her the painting. It was a lovely seascape with her sitting on the sand and looking out at the far horizon, the sunlight on her. It was the only time he had ever painted her. She had said nothing, she had just stood and looked at the wet oils until the scene blurred before her eyes – and then tried to hand him the painting back, but he would not take it.

Aba had the Chinese carpenters who worked in the thatched shed behind the stables carve a lovely gilded frame for the painting and then had it hung in the long hallway of the hacienda, where the light from a south-facing window would illuminate it, as if it were precious. She closed her eyes now and bit at her lower lip.

On the night that she had run away, she had removed the small painting from its place on the wall and took it with her, carried it wrapped in brown paper for three months, carried it for more than 5,000 miles, and did not know why. All she knew was that she wanted it. No – needed it. She had hung it in her cell at the monastery. It didn't matter why.

234

For a time, she watched the sea grass waving in the morning breeze, then she started back.

Sundown at the hacienda had always been her favourite time: the cool dry breezes, the sweet smell of night jasmine, smears of lamplight on dead-white plaster, the river whispering as if it wanted to tell her something. But there was nothing to love about this evening.

She was sitting in a rocker on the veranda next to her father, a thin film of sweat covering her skin, her thoughts focused back on the little pocket in the sand dunes where they had sat together. Don Lugo coughed. She looked at him. He was sitting in a chair, sketching chickens scratching for corn he had tossed into the dirt at the porch edge. He was making sketch after sketch, his hand moving so fast over the paper that it looked as if he were trying to pack a lifetime of drawing into one evening.

She fought back the tears and shook her head. He wore a Mexican general's dress uniform with a purple sash and a fine silver sword. She shook her head again and smiled at the outlandish outfit. It was the first time in her life that she had ever done that: smiled fondly at his craziness.

They had been sitting in silence for the past hour. For all she knew, he was not even aware that she was next to him. There was a growing pile of crumpled papers beside his chair. Then Min came out of the house, approaching slowly in his mincing shuffle, bowing up and down as he came, smiling his forever smile. But as before, she could see the sadness in the boy's features. Aba had told her that the Patrón had found him wandering the streets – an abandoned child of eight or nine – and brought him home to the hacienda where he had lived ever since. He stopped

235

a few feet from the Patrón, bowed deeply and held the position.

'Don Lugo –'

The old man did not respond. He just continued drawing.

Min waited, bent over. Finally, he said, 'Don Lugo, is there anything you wish?'

Sister Ria was stunned by the quickness of her father as he exploded like a coiled snake, knocking his chair backwards and tossing his sketchbook out into the yard, scattering frightened chickens. Then slowly he turned towards the young servant, his hand moving towards the hilt of his sword.

Min was backing and bowing his way towards the house.

'I have told you before, do not disturb me when I am working.'

'Father –'

'You be quiet!' he yelled, whirling and glaring at her. Then he turned back to the frightened boy. 'Do you not know who I am?' he shouted.

Sister Ria was moving to stop him, when Aba appeared in the doorway. 'Don Lugo,' she said firmly, her voice snapping like a flag in the wind.

The old man looked at her, hesitated, then stood glaring down at the bent-over back of Min. Aba watched him for a moment longer, to be sure the tirade was over, and then nodded deferentially and picked up the chair and sketchbook.

The Patrón turned towards her. 'Have the children been fed?' he growled.

'Of course, Don Lugo,' she said, her voice carefully modulated, once again the respectful head servant.

Aba took him by the arm and guided him back to his

chair and handed him his sketchbook, dusting it carefully with her apron before she let it go. The Patrón cleared his throat and pulled a new charcoal pencil from his fine military coat and resumed his frantic sketching – this time of Min's frightened face.

It was fully dark when the horse and carriage came down the long drive and stopped in front of the veranda where Sister Ria and her father were still sitting. The servants had lit the lantern sconces on the hacienda walls an hour earlier and these were casting a weak light onto the faces of Dr Reed Johnson and José Vargas in the carriage. The men nodded at Sister Ria.

'Gentlemen,' she said.

The Patrón did not acknowledge them.

'We have come to speak with Don Lugo,' Vargas said, struggling down from the buggy.

Sister Ria stood. 'I'll leave you,' she said, her voice cold, still not certain what to think of Don Vargas.

Aba had stepped out onto the veranda and stood a few feet away, tall and straight, a black shawl over her shoulders, her thin hands clasped in front of her.

'No,' Vargas said, 'you should hear this.' The old lawyer was using a cane and he hobbled up onto the veranda in front of Don Lugo. He stood for a moment looking down at his old friend. Don Lugo continued to ignore him, staring out into the darkness of the yard as if he were the only person alive in the world. Vargas stepped closer and touched the Patrón's shoulder, then brought the hand tenderly to his face. 'Maxie. It's José Vargas. I've come to tell you that everything legal has been completed and signed by the officials of the city and the state to allow the execution to proceed. I have been asked by the district court of

237

Los Angeles to read you the following order for your execution.'

Sister Ria thought that Aba had taken a step backwards at the words, but she was not certain. The old woman was standing with her chin elevated slightly, her eyes locked on the Patrón. Vargas began to read, but Sister Ria was no longer hearing him. Her mind was being swept along by a brutal flood of memories: hacienda mornings, Milagros, coffee and chocolates, foreign newspapers, arguments, grape harvests. Her breath was jerking in her throat. She stepped up behind her father's chair and put her hands on his shoulders and squeezed slightly. He did not move. Vargas finished.

'Don Lugo,' Dr Johnson said, squatting in front of his chair, 'I am to give you a physical examination. It is a final requirement of the law.' He shook his head. 'Don't ask me why.'

Aba and Sister Ria said in unison, 'No.'

'You will not touch him,' Sister Ria continued.

Johnson stood up and stepped back until he and Vargas were shoulder to shoulder. The physician ran his tongue over his lips and then nodded. 'Looks healthy to me. Don Vargas?'

'To me as well,' Vargas said, softly. 'Strong as a range bull . . . a great man of royal Spanish lineage.'

The servants had brought chairs and trays of coffee and sweets and Vargas and Johnson were sitting in front of Don Lugo, talking about times past. Every so often Don Lugo would nod, but he remained silent, gazing off towards the river and the distant fields beyond. Sister Ria stood holding his thin shoulders and looking down at him, something tearing loose in her chest, breaking up the last of her rigid stubbornness towards this man.

238

When they were ready to leave, Vargas motioned for Sister Ria to follow him. She patted her father's shoulder and joined the old man on the other side of the buggy. Vargas leaned into the carriage for support and handed her an envelope.

'What is it?' her voice was cool.

'The contract for the sale of La Brea.'

She shook her head.

'Listen to me,' he whispered. 'You are young. Sell it. It's only five acres. Take the money and repair La Cienega, turn it into a hospital or a nunnery, or whatever you wish – but do it, child.' He stopped talking and looked across the darkness at his old friend sitting on the chair, Aba standing behind him. 'You can't save him.'

Sister Ria raised her eyebrows. 'And what do you get if I sign it, Don Vargas?'

'I receive nothing,' Vargas said, clearing his throat. 'What did I call you as a child?'

She didn't answer him.

'Isadora,' he said firmly.

'La niña testaruda,' she whispered.

'Yes. But you are no longer a child, Isadora.' He shuffled his feet. 'Your father wants you happy.'

She shook her head slowly. 'My father is mad.'

Vargas studied her face. 'The day you returned, he told me to prepare the documents.'

'What documents?'

'The contract for the sale of La Brea and the transfer of La Cienega to you – for his signature and yours.' He held the papers out to her. 'He has signed it – for you. Now you must do the same – for him.'

Her eyes were closed and she was shaking her head back and forth again, tears running down her cheeks.

*　　*　　*

239

Sister Ria opened the papers Vargas had given her: the signature was clearly her father's. Don Vargas and Reed Johnson had left over an hour ago but she was still struggling to breathe. Aba and the other servants had gone inside, leaving her alone with her father.

She pulled up a chair close in front of him and grasped his hands in hers. He did not pull away, he just sat looking at her. She was fighting for control of her emotions. 'Why?' she moaned. 'Why could we never understand one another?'

She waited for him to answer but he just sat and watched her face.

'What was I to you, Father? Property, like your horses or bulls? Tell me. What was I? For once – just for once – tell me that I am your daughter. Please do that. For me.'

He did not tell her.

She wiped her eyes on the sleeve of her habit and took a deep breath and patted his hand. 'I'm sorry. It's too late for answers. I know that. Let me at least pray with you.'

He shook his head.

She ignored him and moved her chair closer to him and began to pray. He did not resist. His hands were cold. She blew on them and rubbed them to warm them, and prayed – prayed until she could no longer keep her eyes open. She leaned back in her chair and slipped into a deep, exhausted sleep. When the Christ Child came to her again, he said nothing to her, just shook his head – and she understood and whispered, 'I will no longer try to help him, Christ Jesus.' She moaned a moan that sounded like someone was tearing her insides out.

When she awoke, little red bats were flitting in and out under the eaves of the veranda chasing insects near the lanterns. She was sitting in the rocking chair with a blanket draped over her. Aba must have put it there. Her father was gone. Fernando was sitting at her side watching a large moth fluttering against the glass of a wall sconce. She felt a deep melancholy. Then she gasped: her eyes locked on the moth. It was black, the margins of its wings wavy, with two large pink-rimmed spots that looked like eyes on its lower wings – the same creature she had smashed with the broom that night in the alley. She was certain of it.

She shivered and stood up quickly, and the moth, as if sensing her intention, fluttered away into the night. Then it was suddenly back, circling her head in its unsteady flight, as if taunting her, and she was swinging wildly at it, the dark creature swirling in the mad eddies of her swings like a leaf caught in the fast waters of a stream. Then it was gone again.

She stood for a minute, searching the porch and surrounding darkness for it, the house and grounds silent. She shivered and picked up the blanket from the tiles and pulled it over her shoulders. The bats continued their erratic flights under the eaves. The dark sky was speckled with a million stars. Slowly she calmed down.

Standing here in the chill of the night, staring past the old stone fountain to the river and the distant fields, it was as if nothing had changed in her life. Yet everything had changed.

Fernando was trotting ahead of her, his tail stuck arrogantly up in the air, as Sister Ria walked down the darkened hallway of the hacienda towards her room. Suddenly the cat stopped moving and arched his back, his fur rising like it had been charged with electricity, his ears laid flat against his head.

The sound was barely audible – the noise of furniture

being moved, sliding into walls. Sister Ria stood probing the weak light, listening for the vibrations in the air, trying to understand it. Surely Aba was not cleaning another room at this hour. She started walking again. Fernando hung back, then shot ahead of her.

She had almost reached her room when she heard a muffled cry coming from inside and she lunged for the door.

The figure in the brown suit was bent over Estrella's bed, holding the girl pinned under the covers, Estrella kicking and squealing, desperately struggling to get away.

'Leave her alone!' Sister Ria yelled.

The sheer volume of the scream caused the figure to step back from the bed into the darkness and Estrella came out from under the blankets crying hysterically, 'My hands are cut!'

Sister Ria grabbed the girl and shoved her out into the hallway, yanking the bedroom door shut, then whirled around. The figure had moved boldly back towards her. She tried to make out the face in the darkness but could not. Fernando leaped between them, his body swollen, hissing at the dark shape.

'She's just a child!' Sister Ria screamed. 'You tried to kill a child!' Whatever natural fear Sister Ria felt was replaced by wrath that surged up into her throat like vomit. 'May God curse you!'

Sister Ria could see a knife blade glinting weak bolts of light in the dark. 'Put it down!'

But the figure did not put the knife down. Instead it moved slowly towards her. Then suddenly people were running and yelling in the hacienda and the figure darted through the garden door into the night, Fernando and Sister Ria in pursuit.

They ran twisting and turning through the garden, matching each other stride for stride, locked in deadly silent manoeuvring. Whenever the figure slowed, Sister Ria slowed, waiting for her chance to attack, knowing she had to be careful of the knife. Each time they slowed, Fernando would dart ahead and attack the figure, spitting and hissing. They were running again, dodging through the tangled maze of bushes, rose thorns cutting at them.

They were deep in the garden and had stopped again, Sister Ria panting and listening to the old cat waging his fierce battle with the fleeing figure. Then suddenly it was silent. She held her breath and listened. Nothing. No sound except for the blood pounding in her.

Back inside the house, candles and lanterns were being lit in the upstairs rooms as the frantic search for the intruder continued. She edged around a tall, dense oleander bush, holding her breath and probing the night for movement on the other side, her fists clenched. Still nothing.

Common sense told her to back away – that this was a murderer with a knife.

But the anger would not let her.

'Father?'

Silence.

She turned her head slowly back and forth trying to pick up sound in the still night, listening for a twig breaking, a rustling of leaves. But there was nothing.

Sister Ria gathered her courage and lunged around the bush. No one.

Then she saw him.

The old cat was lying under the edge of a towering oleander bush, the intruder gone. Sister Ria knelt and reached out and touched Fernando's shoulder, feeling for a response. He was breathing, but barely. She pulled off her wimple and draped it over him.

'Can you hear me?'

The tom seemed to stir but then went limp again. She moaned deep inside herself. The old cat had fought so hard to protect her and she didn't know why. Nor did she know what to say to him. He had spent his life surviving on his own, fighting for just a place in this world. Had he sensed that same thing in her? Was that why he had so suddenly and fiercely thrown in with her? She had never done much of anything for him that would deserve such fierce loyalty.

She stroked his fur, something she had never been able to do before. The old cat struggled to stand and fell back. Then he twisted his head and bit at the air as if trying to bite an invisible hand.

'It's OK,' she whispered, fighting the choking in her windpipe.

He was almost gone. She cleared her throat and said the only thing that made sense: 'You wait for me in Heaven. Hear? If I get there I'll find you, I promise. And we'll eat every night at the best Italian place in Heaven. But no chasing birds.'

He stopped struggling.

'Fernando?'

She kissed his head.

Then she heard the screeching of the hinges.

The small door in the stone foundation of the hacienda was open. She could see the steps leading down some fifteen feet into La Cienega's root cellar. She stood at the blackened opening and got her bearings before starting down. The cellar was a large rectangle measuring forty by sixty feet. Its roof was the heavy bottom floor of the house, this supported by a single line of large stone pillars running down the centre at ten-foot intervals.

She took a deep breath and held it, peering into the darkness below. There were so many places to hide down there – she and Milagros had played 'Hide and Seek' countless times. Small rooms lined both sides of the long walls of the rectangle – rooms used for storing produce and canned goods for the hacienda's winter use: rooms where he could be waiting. She let her breath go and quickly took another. There was a second door at the far end of the rectangle that opened out on the service road. But it was kept locked by Aba to prevent pilfering by the workers. Few knew where the key was hidden.

Sister Ria started down the steps, stumbling at the bottom, and then forcing herself to scramble through the pitch blackness of the rooms on one side of the cellar. Her breath heaved. Empty. She was just starting to cross to the other side to check the rooms there when she heard the sound of something moving in the darkness. Then it was still again. She trembled and wanted to turn and flee but could not.

She pulled herself up straight and squared her shoulders, sensing something in the darkness. Whoever it was, they were standing in the shadows nearby. Instinctively, she moved through the black gloom until she touched the heavy stone pillar in the centre of the room, backing up against it for protection, held her breath and opened her mouth slightly and listened again. She jumped. Off to her right, one of the glass canning jars had fallen shattering over the floor. Frightened, she pressed harder into the stones of the pillar and waited.

Then she heard the whisper. It hissed at her, mocking

her: 'Holy Sister – help me. Please.' It was the same voice she had heard in the alley, the same voice outside her door. Anger rose burning in her throat.

'Go to Hell!' she shouted.

The room fell silent again.

Long minutes passed before she felt more than heard another movement, and canted her head towards it. Something was stirring in the darkness. There was a small window high up the wall opposite her and a soft beam of moonlight spilled in onto the floor. Again she heard a sound. Closer this time. She balled her fists. Then she saw a large dark shape dart across the light, and she sucked all the air she could into her lungs. Ready to fight.

Sister Ria was trying to hear, or see, or sense something that would tell her where the figure had gone. Should she move? No, that would give away her position. As she was worrying these thoughts, the sickening realization suddenly came to her: she was now alone in the cellar. The figure had escaped out the second door!

'No!' she cried.

Sister Ria whirled and desperately felt with her hands over the cold surface of the heavy pillar: the small stone near the top was missing. She was gasping for breath. Aba kept the key behind that stone. She began to pound on the rocks of the pillar, a long, low wailing sob coming from somewhere deep inside her.

Frantically, she retraced her steps, knocking over baskets of produce, falling and getting up and running again, her feet bounding up the stairs, back out into the night and the garden. Once in the open, she broke into a hard run. She went past the stone gazebo, up the wide flight of marble stairs, down a narrow passageway behind the work sheds, and slid to a stop. The second door was still shut.

Her heart was pounding in her ears. It was all she could hear now.

She rocked back and forth on her feet, her fists, still covered with Estrella's blood, clenching and unclenching. She stiffened with grim determination when she heard the key turn in the rusty lock. What seemed an eternity passed before the small rear door to the root cellar slowly opened, and the figure in the brown suit stepped out into the night.

'Why?' Sister Ria said.

The figure jumped slightly at the sound of her voice.

'Why?' she repeated, the word more a moan than a question.

The figure in the brown suit was holding a small derringer in one hand. Sister Ria did not care. She stepped closer. 'Why?'

The figure reached up and yanked off the fedora and sailed it into the night. Milagros' beautiful black hair fell over her shoulders. 'What don't you understand, little sister?'

'None of it.'

Milagros' eyes narrowed. 'You have been in the convent too long.'

'That's not an answer!'

'You want an answer?' Milagros hissed. 'I'll give you one. Two years ago my husband threw me out so that he could move a goddamned prostitute into my house! Can you understand that? I was tossed out onto the streets of San Francisco with nothing. Nothing.'

Sister Ria watched her.

'He threw me out so he could move in a whore. I was a Mexican divorcee in the Anglo city of San Francisco. Do you know what that means?' She was shaking her head and breathing hard. Sister Ria did not answer. 'No,

I didn't think you did. It means I might as well have been dead.'

Sister Ria pressed the palms of her hands together and closed her eyes.

'Don't give me your damn prayers, Isadora.'

Sister Ria ignored her.

'I had nothing – so I turned to our beloved father. You know him, the father who tried to turn you into a man.'

Sister Ria continued praying.

'Look at me, dammit!'

Sister Ria opened her eyes, the palms of her hands still pressed together in front of her face. When she finally spoke, her voice was low and firm. 'Millie, you killed a woman and her baby.'

'I don't want your morality.'

Aba was calling Sister Ria's name in the distance.

Milagros paced back and forth in front of her. 'You know what our dear father said when I asked for help? He said: "Come back to La Cienega."' Milagros waved an arm at the darkness. 'He welcomed me back to all this: a house of mud, life as an old maid, with that bitch of a servant harping at me. How wonderfully kind.' Her voice was laced with disdain. 'He welcomed me back to the same two-bit town that I ran from. That you ran from, don't you forget.' Milagros shook her head. 'I wasn't coming back. No matter what, I wasn't coming back.'

'He welcomed you home, Milagros.' She paused. 'That's all he had to offer.'

Milagros laughed. 'Home to all this splendour.' She shook her head. 'I asked him for money, he gave me a hundred dollars. Every month Vargas wired a hundred lousy dollars!'

Sister Ria just stared at her sister.

Milagros shook her head. 'A maid costs a hundred dollars. I asked him for a thousand – and he gave me a hundred.'

'He's lost almost everything, Millie.'

'I'm not a fool, Izzie. I know that,' she said, unbuttoning the brown cutaway jacket. 'So when the gas company wanted to buy La Brea I begged him to sell.'

Sister Ria's voice sounded distant. 'So he could pay you more?'

'I was desperate! I was his daughter. I had put up with his madness for all those years. He owed me that!'

'You killed her because she was a prostitute.'

'Don't be stupid, Izzie. I killed her because I knew a Mexican killing a white woman was going away for life. So I left his things in her room, certain the cretins they call police in this town would arrest him. And I was just as certain Dearly Deranged would act like a madman and get himself convicted.'

'He is our father,' Sister Ria moaned.

'Don't pull your holy crap with me, Isadora. I stood up to him for you too many times for you to pull that on me!'

'Why?' Sister Ria sobbed.

'Because once he was gone I was going to own this grand pile of mud.' She shook her head. 'He likes play-acting – and he played this one superbly. Only he played it too well and they condemned him to death.' She shook her head. 'That was his doing, not mine.'

Sister Ria shuddered, suddenly unable to speak.

'I knew the court would award La Cienega to us.' Milagros laughed and looked at her sister's face. 'And I never thought you'd come back.'

'She was going to have a child.'

'A bastard, you mean?'

Sister Ria was not listening. She was gazing into the shadows on the ground, remembering the times they had played dolls with their nursemaids, collected shells along the beach, raced their ponies, fished for crayfish in the river. Her heart had never left those days. She looked up slowly at Milagros, focusing hard on her sister's face. Her words, when she finally found her voice, were woven with deep, sorrowful pain.

'You thought it was me in the bed tonight. Didn't you, Millie? You thought it was me and you were going to kill me.'

Milagros did not hesitate. 'Yes.'

Sister Ria closed her eyes.

'Yes,' Milagros repeated.

'Oh, Millie –'

'You did this to yourself,' Milagros said. 'I told you to leave.'

Milagros pulled the brown suit jacket off and tossed it on the ground. 'I tried to scare you off by killing that chicken and then putting the dead child in the crib . . . and all the rest. But Your Holiness had to stay and meddle.' She paused. 'And then I realized that you were just like him – that you would get stubborn and undo everything. And I was right, wasn't I?' Milagros was shaking her head, her dark hair flying in the night air. 'So don't you blame me. You brought this on yourself.'

When she spoke, Sister Ria's voice sounded distant. 'When I was a child, you stood up for me. And you were just a child yourself – young but so very brave. And I loved you.'

250

'That doesn't matter now.'

'Yes it does, Millie. It will always matter.'

Milagros cocked the hammer on the little pistol. 'Turn around, Izzie.'

Sister Ria shook her head. 'No.' She inhaled a deep breath. 'You'll see my face. You'll see what we once were to each other.' Sister Ria stopped talking and shook her head, 'I won't turn.'

'Turn!' Milagros snapped.

Sister Ria was crying now. She made a sweeping gesture with her hand and bowed at the waist. 'I present the Great La Conquistadora. She fears nothing.' When she straightened up, Milagros was pointing the pistol at her.

'That was a child's game, Izzie.'

'It was our game. What we believed. Rueque para su alma.'

'He wouldn't help me,' Milagros moaned. 'I tried to get work. But I don't know how to work. The only thing I could do was clean people's houses. That's all.' She stared at Sister Ria's face. 'I cleaned houses for two years. I washed floors and rich Americans' filthy undergarments. And they treated me like I was trash. I couldn't do that any more, Izzie. I couldn't. You understand.'

'I don't.'

'Turn around, Izzie.'

Sister Ria broke a rose from a nearby bush and tossed it at Milagros' feet. 'Take it with you when you're done. La Rosa de Castilla. To remember us.' Milagros looked down briefly at the rose, then up at her sister's face. And for an instant her features seemed to soften, and Sister Ria thought she looked like La Conquistadora once again.

251

Aba's voice was growing louder.

The shot from the derringer blew the hair out on one side of Milagros' head, like a small puff of wind.

ONE DAY . . .

NINETEEN

The Mexican part of the city was a dusty shade of taupe, but there were green places, and Sister Ria was sitting on a bench near the old pueblo fountain gazing at one, the tendrils of an ancient creeper that spread over an adobe wall like the thick fingers of a moss-coloured hand, staring as if she could see people moving in the vine, remembering her sister, and praying for forgiveness for both their souls.

She stirred. Don José Vargas' servant, Antonio Mollena, was hurrying up the road towards her, holding out an envelope. 'Señora. Don Vargas has spoken to the Governor.'

'Thank you.'

The man dipped his head and walked quickly away. Vargas had left on the morning train for Sacramento to see the Governor, to tell him there was proof of Don Lugo's innocence.

She ran a finger under the envelope's flap. '*Doña Isadora: Don Maximiato's jornado del muerto will continue. Vargas.*' The journey of death, Sister Ria thought.

Sister Ria and Aba were marching shoulder to shoulder down the loggia of the hacienda, headed for Don Lugo's room, when they saw the children – Min, Estrella, Cristina and the orphans in their new shoes, all of them standing in two long lines against both walls of the wide hallway. They were crying. Estrella stepped forward carrying a large tin pail stuffed with roses in her bandaged hands.

'For the Patrón,' she sniffed. 'We each picked one.'

'Thank you, children,' Sister Ria said. 'They will make him very happy.'

Estrella started to sob.

'Hush,' Aba said sternly, 'you have work to do. Min, make the children do their work. I will inspect it later.'

The two women started off down the hall again, turning a corner and approaching a young policeman Hood had posted at the Patrón's bedroom door that morning. The man was sitting on a chair. He jumped up and yanked off his cap when he saw the old woman. Then he looked at Sister Ria dressed in her stark black-and-white habit and quickly crossed himself. 'Ladies,' he said in a voice that broke into a squeak. 'My orders are to check you for weapons.'

Sister Ria stopped. Aba did not. The old woman grabbed Sister Ria by the arm and marched her around the boyish-looking policeman.

'You will check nothing,' Aba snapped, 'you are a guest in the house of the Patrón.'

'I guess not,' the young man mumbled.

Don Lugo was sitting in the centre of his bedroom painting at his easel. He was dressed in a bright red toreador's outfit, the sequins reflecting the lamplight as though they were scales on a large red fish, his spindly calves covered in white gauzy stockings, black slippers on his feet. As he did on the previous night on the veranda, he was working fast.

256

Sister Ria stepped behind him and put a hand on his shoulder. 'Father, it is Isadora.'

'I do not want to pray,' he said.

'Then I will pray for you.'

He did not respond. He was painting what looked like a woman, the body clothed in a dark dress, the head not yet brushed onto the canvas. She leaned close to him and whispered, 'At least tell me that I am your daughter.' Her voice broke with emotion. 'At least do that so that I can forgive –'

He continued painting.

She pulled a stool close to him and sat and took a deep breath. 'Surely you remember our life together.' She began to tell him everything she could about their lives here. Big and small things – good things: about the great horse Cibola, about the mornings when they had sat together in the cafés drinking coffee and arguing with the men of the pueblo about the world and life. She told him about her mother and brother, about Milagros when she was a girl. She did not tell him about Milagros' death nor what Milagros had done. She would let God do that. She told him how proud she had been when he bought the children's shoes and when he had buried Dorothy Regal's child. She remembered for him the day he had painted her on the beach. She told him that she had kept the painting with her ever since.

She talked to him for more than two hours. Don Lugo continued to paint. But she sensed he was listening. She took the brush gently from his hand and turned him on his stool so that he was facing her, and grasped both of his hands, cleared her throat and said, 'I am your daughter. Please, at least say that.'

He looked at her face and their eyes held for a moment.

257

Then he turned back to the easel and swirled a brush in a can of thinner and wiped it clean on a rag, and said nothing.

'Father –' she said, her voice breaking.

'Can you not see that I am working?'

Sister Ria wiped at her eyes and smiled. 'Yes, Father.'

It was done.

He went back to his painting. Sister Ria went to Aba.

'I have said what I wanted to say,' she whispered. 'Now you must.'

Aba shook her head and Sister Ria could see that the old woman was worrying her hands.

'You must do it now,' she hissed.

'Silencio!' he snapped, dabbing his brush in a gob of green paint on his mixing board.

Sister Ria looked at Aba, raised her eyebrows and nodded fiercely in the direction of her father. The old woman walked slowly towards him.

Sister Ria was moving to the back of the room to give Aba privacy, when she saw it. The door to the small room was cracked open a few inches. She heard Aba say his name and she pushed the door open and stepped inside, closing it behind her. No light was burning in this room, but there was a small oval window at one end that let in the sun's light. The compartment was a small rectangle, some twelve feet by twenty.

Sister Ria let her eyes adjust to the shadows, trying not to listen to the muffled sound of Aba's voice. Her eyes scanned the walls. And suddenly, she wanted to sit down.

It was a gallery of his paintings.

They hung on the walls, covering every inch of space. In addition, there were stacks of other canvases leaning against the walls of the room. Hundreds of them. But that was not what caused her to stand with her mouth open. It was the paintings themselves. It was as if the Lugo family had suddenly come alive around her. There were pictures of her mother, Milagros, Ramón and herself. Dozens of paintings. Paintings of her and her siblings at different ages, from babies, to youngsters, to young adults.

Sister Ria pressed her hands to her mouth. She had never seen any of these, had never seen him working on any of them. He had carefully observed his children and wife, made mental notes about colouring and moods, then retired to the solitude of his room to paint them into liquid life. They were wonderful paintings, capturing individual moods and personalities. Most amazing of all, this man who had such a difficult time relating to his family had painted himself into each canvas in close, loving poses – an arm around a shoulder, a hand on an arm, gazing proudly at his children, his smiling face haunting the shadowy background of a portrait.

Her eyes locked on a picture of herself as a young child sitting at the library table. She was reading, unaware that he was standing in a doorway behind her, gazing fondly at her. She began to cry. Then she abruptly stopped and gazed into the weak light of the room. The memory of the vision she'd had of the Christ Child was drifting through her thoughts. 'Do not help him,' the Child had said. 'Do not.'

Sister Ria stumbled around the room, 'Please, Jesus, please.' She sat on a small stool, rocking back and forth in her agony. Then she looked up at a painting of her as a child of eleven or twelve, her father's arm around her shoulder. They were both smiling. Sister Ria stood and took the painting from the wall.

She opened the door and walked out into the room. He was still working at his easel. Aba nodded at her. She returned the nod and, clutching the painting against her breast, walked over and put a hand to her father's cheek. He didn't react.

She studied his face for a long time – wanting to remember him for all time. Finally she drew in a sharp breath that hurt and held the painting out in front of him. 'Father, look at it. Who is that?' She pointed at the child in the picture. 'Who? Tell me!'

He said nothing. And Sister Ria stood and looked down at the top of his head, wiping the tears from her cheeks on her habit.

When she was convinced he would not respond, she said, 'Father, I pray for both our souls that we will see each other again in Heaven and we can talk more.' She hesitated, 'Perhaps we will understand each other then.'

He continued painting.

She had turned and was walking slowly towards the door when she heard it. 'Daughter –' he mumbled. It felt as if God had touched her, again, as He had that day so long ago in the sea. She turned and stared at her father. He was still painting.

'Thank you,' she said.

That was when she made her decision.

The young policeman jumped up from his chair and backed nervously away as the old woman and the nun marched out of Don Lugo's room and down the loggia. 'Have a good evening, ladies,' he called. Neither of them turned around. He shrugged again.

Chief Raymond Hood, determined to avoid trouble with the crowds of Mexicans gathering on the road to La

Cienega, had come early with his deputies, entering the Patrón's bedroom at 3.30 a.m. It was dark and chilly.

Don Lugo was sitting alone in front of his easel, staring at the fresh canvas, as the deputy cuffed his hands behind him. Hood looked at the painting and shook his head. The man had painted his old servant – making her look almost special.

'Morning, Max,' he said.

The Patrón ignored him.

'You ready, Rojo?' Hood yelled out the door.

The young newspaper editor had been hired by the sheriff to photograph the proceedings, purportedly to document things. But Clemente Rojo figured it was as much an election ploy on the part of the police chief. Even so, he would do it and run the photos in *La Verdad*. He had photographed the original murder scene, Don Lugo when he was arrested, the trial, the jury, Don Lugo convicted, and now he would photograph the man's execution. To honour the man.

'Rojo!'

'Yes, I'm ready.'

'Good.' Hood turned and looked at Don Lugo. 'You want a cigarette?'

Don Lugo shook his head.

'You want to write anything?'

He did not respond. Hood stood looking down at him, thinking that the man was dressed appropriately: black boots, black pants, a waist-length black cape, a black silk scarf wound around his neck and up over half his face against the chill, and a black gaucho hat that was pulled low.

'Damn it, Rojo, let's get this going,' Hood said.

The editor ignored him and respectfully took off his hat

and said in Spanish, 'May God bless and keep you, Don Lugo.'

Don Lugo said nothing.

'Let's get on with it,' Hood barked. The police chief turned back to the Patrón. 'Well, I guess this is the end of the fiesta, Don. We thought we'd get a photograph of you and me together.'

He adjusted his bow tie and quickly combed his silver hair.

Hood waited until Rojo was ready and then he turned and pulled Don Lugo's scarf off and stood staring open-mouthed into Sister Ria's face.

The photograph was excellent.

Out in the bay of San Pedro lay a ship with her sails unfurled. The morning was still dark, but a thin strip of pink was etching the tops of the San Gabriel Mountains east of Los Angeles. All but two of the people on deck were sailors. The ship's captain, a weathered-looking Irishman in his late sixties, with silver hair, a long stemmed pipe in his mouth, was standing beside these two.

Aba was gazing towards the land. 'How long will it take?' she asked.

'This time of year, with stops in Buenos Aires and Havana, I'd say we'll make Spain in seven weeks.'

The nun standing next to Aba was chain-smoking cigarettes and looking with an appraising eye at the captain's clothing. Unable to contain himself any longer, the nun sidled up next to the man and said, 'I like your hat, Captain.'

The captain looked down at the nun, who had a three-day growth of stubble on his chin, and said, 'Thanks.'

The nun cleared his throat, took a quick draw on his

cigarette and leaned closer to the captain and whispered, 'I'm not really a nun.'

'I guessed that.'

'Good. Do you like this outfit I'm wearing?'

'Don Lugo, it is time for your rest,' Aba said, taking the old man's arm and walking him down the deck.

The wind was picking up.